The Secret Of Harragar

a mythological journey of a
young woman coming of age

Cynthia Loulan Innes

for my husband Geoffrey and the Sunday Writers:
Georgie, Lesley, Marti and Nena

Table of Contents

CHAPTER 1   GRATACO

Limestone cliffs hold the small town of Grataco above its walls like a balancing act. The wind blows hot across the desert in summer, needle sharp in winter. Today the clouds unfold like sheets thrown across an endless blue mattress while the hills to the east are obscured by heat haze.

She needed this place to think, had sat all afternoon dangling her legs over the cliff, gazing down at the plain beneath her in the hope her mind would change course. The wind picked up, blowing her hair across her face which she kept flicking back. She twisted a handful of the long black strands through her fingers, feeling tempted to take out her knife, setting it free with a few deft cuts, but that was not the way of the women of Grataco.

She gazed down at the road zigzagging its way to the bridge over the Sanluz River and wished she was an eagle that could soar above these confines. Where the river flowed into Lake Grataco, the afternoon light made it shimmer like a silver spoon. The pines which shaded the small cabins at the end of the lake began to sway and even though the sun was beginning to lose its intensity, the midsummer wind was still warm, drying her skin like parchment. She continued to sit until the distant peaks began to turn gold signaling it was time for her to leave, but she felt stitched to the rocks, reluctant to return home to see again the concern on the faces of her parents, for she knew she had failed them.

*

She thought back on what had happened this morning. She had known too well what was to follow, for her birthday had just passed and there was no turning back. As she sat out on the back wall she had heard her mother busying herself inside waiting for Poppo to arrive home. He never returned for lunch as he remained up with the goat herds this time of year so she guessed what was afoot. As soon as his gangly figure was seen striding down the hill, Marthamum came out carrying her thick wooden comb, saying "You are no longer a girl now, Prêtzova," and her heart had sunk.

Marthamum had begun to unplait her hair and as she tried to pull away, she felt the firm hand of her father on her shoulder so was forced to remain still until her mother finished brushing out the stubborn strands.

"Now can I go?" she had pleaded, but Marthamum had simply disappeared inside while her father sat silently appraising her until her mother returned with the gown. It was of the softest blue with fine white lace edging the sleeves. It had buttons fashioned from mother of pearl and the edge of the hem had been hand embroidered in the finest of silk thread by her paternal grandmother Varsla, taking the role of Marthamum's mother who had died of the typhus many years past. Pretzel had pushed it away wishing her parents could only see she was not ready to come of age, but there was to be no argument as her mother deftly slipped it over her head. Marthamum had hugged her before stepping back to admire her.

"How can I run in this?" she had protested

"You will grow used to it my dear."

Drako had then stomped up the steps to see her and when his thick black mop of hair fell over his eyes, Marthamum just laughed and ruffled it up more.

"You don't make a fuss about his being in a mess," Pretzel had complained.

"What's wrong with my big sister?"

"She doesn't want to grow up yet."

"Marthamum!" It isn't that! I don't want to be a child and be bossed around forever, but I can't change who I am. I am just not comfortable wearing this."

"When you learn to walk with small quick steps, you will glide like a swan. Here! Let me attach your headdress."

The circle of thick felt sat snuggly on her head, from which draped a deep blue silk scarf.

"A gift from Reza."

She felt more defeated as Marthamum then rearranged her hair around her shoulders which mingled with the blue of the head dress.

Pretzel, born five years before her brother was long and slender with fingers made for harp playing. Then Drako arrived, strong boned, square jawed and with the roar of a lion. He had only to apply his irresistible charm to ask for whatever he wanted.

"Drako will not have to stop living a life when he reaches my age."

Poppo had then stated firmly, "Who can argue with our traditions when no one starves or dies alone, not like other places in the world. You will soon begin to see reason my girl. Our ways are best for everyone."

Pretzel had heard the women talk about the ones that tried to change the ways of Grataco and how they were gently brought back in to line, for greatest of all was the fear of being an outcast without husband or family.

"I am going for a walk. I am upsetting you both too much and …I'll have to try."

With that Pretzel had picked up her skirts and hastened down the steps without looking back. She heard Poppo calling out, "Visit my mother. She will want to see you."

*

The sun had almost set by the time Pretzel climbed back down the steep incline which was treacherous without daylight. She tripped her way past the cliff homes with their tiny front patios from which hung baskets of geraniums glowing deep crimson in the twilight.

"These streets are so beautiful! Why am I so dissatisfied? The others are content with their lot," she muttered to herself, cringing when she pictured her father's disappointed expression when she had hurried out the door. She passed the familiar smells of garlic and barbecued goat as her steps echoed against the stone walls where she followed the maize of paths that led her to her grandmother's house. Already the old woman was waiting outside with a large package. Her apron was splattered with icing sugar and flour. Her faded brown eyes lit up.

"Hi Prêtzova! So you are a woman at last. Just look at you! Oh, if my poor old fine hair could grow again like yours."

She fingered Pretzel's hair before kissing her on both cheeks.

"And take these to your mother to celebrate. She must be well proud. Hurry on now before its dark and tell my son I have almost finished his fiesta shirt. "

"I will tell Poppo."

Old Varsla was not only a seamstress of note, but the best baker in town. Pretzel gathered up the flat bread which was still warm from the oven and forced a smile of thanks as she kicked away at the hem of her dress.

"My girl, you will tear it. Just glide my dear."

She passed the home of the two Matzo brothers who leant over their wall and called out to her, throwing pieces of piecrust which landed in the top of her head dress. Normally Pretzel would have laughed and rebuked them, throwing back up one of Varsla's oat cakes, but she now no longer knew how she could behave as before. It was as though she had in minutes been split asunder.

Marthamum met Pretzel at the door.

"Is Varsla well?"

"Yes. She cooked these for you."

"I have heard you were seen climbing up to your usual place. It is no longer wise. You are a grown woman now and it does not suit to give the impression of idleness."

"Marthamum!"

"We won't argue now my dear for we are leaving soon to eat in the Square. Look at the back of your gown! It is already is covered in dust."

It was only two weeks until the Midsummer Lake Fest. Most people started to celebrate days before, so each night would build up with more and more entertainment in preparation for the Big One as they called it, always bigger and better than the year before.

Poppo returned from the fields and sat on the wall pulling off his boots. He smelt of fresh goat's milk intermingled with mud. As he scrubbed off the mountain dirt which stuck to his hands, he looked round at his family.

"Well pretty Pretz. Are you beginning to accept your transformation, heh?"

Pretzel looked away fighting back tears.

"Listen, my beloved daughter! I am right proud of you, and so is Marthamum. You can sit with the women now."

Pretzel knew she must now greet the older women as equals. She must admire their embroidered scarves and enquire about their intricate designs. She must sit and walk with care. She must not greet their husbands before they acknowledge her. There were suddenly so many rules to remember, but then she also she remembered that she was permitted to share their berry liqueurs and her spirits lifted slightly. She hoped that soon Marko would start up his accordion and she might forget for a while the dark thoughts that kept invading her sleep.

Poppo put his arm through Pretzel and led her down past the avenue of lilacs to the Square followed by Marthamum and Drako. The stalls were already set out displaying meat on skewers covered in herbs and rich sauces, alongside a pile of flat bread.

Marko had finished eating and was starting to tune up. His coin collecting hat was placed in front of him in readiness as he shooed away one of the possum dogs which snuffled under his feet looking for tidbits. Legend goes that these red furred creatures were so called on account of their bushy tails and unusually large eyes. How and when they arrived no one could remember. None of the surrounding towns had them as pets but here they were to stay. There used to be arguments in the Square about who would mind them so it was finally decreed that they were to belong to the center of the town where there would be plenty of food and shelter, and each person could enjoy them. But if a person was left bereft, or dying, or alone for any particular reason, they were allowed to possess one for exactly twelve months, the prescribed length of mourning.

There was the sound of a fiddle in the distance which became louder until the player, a young girl called Tanisha, joined the accordionist. A cluster of clean shirted youths with polished faces stood and watched the violinist who flushed as she played on. Old Devko was dressed in his usual clown costume as children screamed and bantered around him for the biggest of balloons and the stickiest of sweets. He led the dancers in to the centre of the Square while the old folk continued to fuss about Pretzel, clucking and fingering her lace sleeves. Eventually she managed to extract herself and join her friends Dashika and Romela who were flushed with the excitement at the thought of soon becoming of age.

"I can't wait to have my hair hanging out long like yours," Dashika exclaimed.

Pretzel shrugged and shook her head leaving them bewildered as she ran off to join the dancing, tripping over her hem as old Varsla chuckled, "She will learn in due course."

The musicians played a jig and Pretzel wondered how she would ever cope. It was now so different from the high kicks she did with her brother at home. The slow polka was easier when Poppo joined her, taking her arm and for a moment she felt a proud queen, but when the final dance, the intricate steps of the Bratura began she again felt a surge of anger at being so restrained as her gown kept getting in the way of her feet and she felt eyes looking at her. She wanted to crawl into a hole.

Their parents needed to leave before them for this was grape picking time on the high hills above Grataco and the days were long. Poppo's wine was much revered and so this family lived well. Their house had another storey as did Reza's next door and on top of that the roof garden. The sandstone walls were adorned with tiny blue and white tiles carried from way beyond the mountains of Tarzon. The floors were covered in rugs imported from a city even more north and sold by merchants who spoke a different tongue and for which Poppo paid handsomely in large barrels of his well pressed vintage.

When it was time to return home Pretzel searched for Drako, finding him asleep on a bench with a possum dog nestled alongside him. As she lifted the dog away, he woke protesting and staggered up the hill.

They both peered into their parents' room. Marthamum was snoring loudly, one plump arm falling over the side of the bed, while Poppo's chin glistened with saliva in the moonlight.

Pretzel slid into her bed which was covered in a thick goats' wool blanket, for even in summer the Grataco nights could suddenly become chilled by the desert winds. She curled into a ball, listening to the insect hum outside and watching the moon which was about to sink behind the mountains. Far above her was the faint bleating of goats as she tossed and turned, but the thumps in her head were becoming louder. She felt as if black silk threads were pulling her lids open as she waited until the stars dimmed and the distant peaks became purple then pink. Only then could she sleep.

*

Reza, the widow from next door, was up already, carrying her loom out to the patio. For the past thirty years she had been the village weaver, spinning the goats' wool before weaving the heavy rugs of Grataco. But what she enjoyed the most was to dye the silk which she obtained from the town of Sharook. This year her favourite colour was blue until one night one of the Matzo boys had crept into Reza's house to drop a bottle of yellow ochre into the vats. From then on the only choice was green until the carnival season, when out of her containers she pulled her special purple, red and orange silks which sold at a hefty price. This explains why Reza owned the most magnificent hill trolley of all of Grataco which she now hired out after decreeing she was too old to risk her limbs. This did not stop her from watching the young ones careering down the hill, often finishing up in the River Sanluz, but her sturdy trolley always survived its rocky landing.

Pretzel continued to lie there with her eyes closed, listening to Reza's high-pitched singing until Drako yanked her hair.

"They have left for the vineyards hours ago."

Pretzel splashed her face, found the new grey school dress which had been laid out by Marthamum, and threw on the head-dress, now bedecked in a red scarf. She packed two thick bread slices with chunks of cheese before catching up with her brother. She could pick out the students who came from the school of Lafaz at the northern end of Grataco. They joined her school to study the classics and mathematics, but as they had no access to Reza's dyes they stood out in their stark whites. The bell rang, echoing throughout the walls, and the possum dogs scampered towards the gates to sit in wait for their lunchtime tidbits.

"I am following along the track. I must continue to go on even if they lead me across the desert."

"What's the matter, Pretz?"

"Oh nothing, Drako. I couldn't sleep. It must be too much excitement from the carnival. Give me one of your oranges and I will feel better."

"The winged creatures are leading me under the steep cliffs"

"Sure you're alright, Pretz?"

"It's nothing."

Drako turned towards his classes but kept glancing back at his sister until she disappeared through the doors.

The day dragged on for Pretzel and she was relieved to walk up the hill alone, leaving Drako with his hill trolley. She lay on the couch with her eyes closed until Drako arrived, his black hair damp with sweat. He rested his head on her chest, felt the lumps that weren't there last year and shifted down. They both lay there in silence until laughter rang out and there was the sound of feet slithering down the path.

"Yoo hoo! I came home early to see how my grown up girl impressed her teachers and look! Franko has given us some of his ricotta."

Marthamum removed it from a cloth bundle.

"Let's try some now while it is still warm. Drako! Slice up some bread... You look pale, Pretzi."

"I'm fine Marthamum. Just let me be."

"I am walking towards desert cacti, on and on. My spirit flags are calling me."

"What is the matter with you, my precious daughter?"

Pretzel gazed into her mother's face, at her untroubled skin that had never known darkness.

"Oh it's nothing."

Marthamum had never been to the higher classes for she had opted to plant vines, wander with the goatherds and feel the wind. But she knew times had changed and daughters needed to Know Things. Poppo had agreed it was important that Pretzel Knew Things although after seeing Pretzel's reaction that morning she wondered now if she was just making her daughter more confused and discontent.

"It's not the mathematics, and the students from Lafaz are funny. I like them. It's not that, Marthamum."

"Ah. I know! You love the mountains too much," Marthamum said soothingly, "but did you not say you wanted to learn more. Learn about trigonometry and the stars that I never had a chance to learn about?"

Drako watched Pretzel's face closely. He knew her sister's every facial twitch and every lip quiver, for she had spent so much time caring for him when their parents arrived home exhausted.

To him Pretzel was his Saviour. He guessed that it wasn't the school or the long garments that worried her so greatly.

"Pretz, what is it?" he whispered, as they washed their hands in the bathroom.

"I can't tell you just now."

Pretzel looked out at the painting of her Aunt Lena. She was sitting by the lake, dangling her feet in the water. Her dress hung in neat folds around her. They said Pretzel was meant to be like her: tall, elegant, and...very proper.

"They are singing to me now. Do not turn away."

"They are telling me, Drako."

"Who?"

"My flags are becoming louder. I thought at first they came in my dreams, but now by day. In class. In the café. People keep saying, 'What's the matter Pretzel. You are not with us.' I am scared, Drako."

"Ricotta on the table," sang out Marthamum, her plump arms cutting it into thick chunks. The bread was warm and buttery. Red wine, diluted with cool lake water stood on the table in a glazed pot. Poppo stomped in singing to himself in a guttural voice as she looked up.

"You timed it well, Poppovosko!"

Poppo ate hungrily, glancing at his daughter.

"Right, Pretz. What did you learn today?"

"Nothing much, Poppo. Some trigonometry. You have shown me that already."

Marthamum caught Poppo's eye.

"She isn't happy."

Pretzel could no longer bear another night of torment. She took a breath.

"I'm leaving, Poppo."

Poppo dropped his fork.

"Giving up already? That's not like you. Or are you following in Marthamum's footsteps?"

"I need my rucksack, the drinking bottle and the red cocoon sac to sleep in."

Poppo put his head in his hands remembering night after night his own private battle. Everyone knew all Gratacians were aware of those who had been pulled away leaving the safety of their village and once gone never returned. Everyone knew once their minds were made up, not a soul could stop them. There was talk of swollen rivers, of ships bearing one away on massive waves. There was more talk of desert thirst and of terrifying creatures in the mountains. Their names were not mentioned again for it was too unbearable to think of. Poppo looked up to see his daughter's determined face and went pale, remembering as a small boy the tall figure walking away into the darkness.

Drako looked into the eyes of his sister and knew that she was already lost to him. His jaw became squarer, his feet rocked to and fro under the table and his eyes widened to contain the brimming tears. He sat, breath barely perceptible, willing his sister to change her mind.

CHAPTER 2   THE LAKE FEST

Reza sat in her roof garden with her spinning wheel, surrounded by her bags of goats' wool. There was no usual sound of the gate swinging open which heralded Poppo's departure and her signal to wave to him. She leant over the railing.

"Is everything alright in there, Poppovosko Dubajka?"

There was not a sound. She put on her slippers and ran lightly down the side steps to the wall to call out again but there was no answer. Being always the first to know any gossip in the town, she rushed into her bedroom to attach her headdress and when she knocked on the door Poppo answered.

"We are really fine, Reza. It was the late night and we are all a bit sick. Thank you for your concern."

She found the door closing politely in front of her and guessed there must be more to it than that. Her neighbours both had the resilience of an ox. She returned to her small kitchen to brew her special blend of herbal tea and this time let her self in through the back door to find Marthamum sitting back on the cushions looking pale.

"This will cure your sickness, my dear."

'Thank you Reza, but I am not unwell."

"Then what can it be?"

This was greeted with silence. Reza gave a shrug and sensing her presence was not required left quickly and returned to her loom, her curiosity getting the better of her as she spun as she listened for any sound from her neighbours.

*

"You try, Drako," Marthamum whispered.

Drako walked over to his sister, scrutinizing her face until she could bear it no longer.

"No one can persuade me to stay for I no longer belong here. They have called me, Drako, and now I must…."

"Shhh, sister. You are not going to leave me. You can't."

Poppo went outside to check that Reza was out of earshot and returned to sit beside Pretzel who could sense his whole body trembling.

"Your mother wills you to change your mind."

"I have come of age now and no one can hold me back. You know that, Poppo!"

"What about me, Pretzi!"

"She is confused by her spirit flags, Drako. She will eventually see reason."

But Drako knew his sister too well, as he plunked down on the kitchen chair, continually tapping his foot on the floor.

"We must do what we can to persuade her out of these crazy thoughts."

"Don't speak as if I am not here, Poppo. It is all darkness at present. I cannot see into my future any more than you can, but these are my flags talking. Mine alone."

Marthamum pulled her daughter to her, her mouth quivering so much she could barely speak.

"You can be a child again. You can plait your hair and take off the gown. I would do anything…"

Pretzel shook her head. Marthamum followed Pretzel's gaze out the window at the flame trees which were suddenly lit up by the morning sun which turned them blood red.

"'Just look at this place, daughter! How can you throw it away!"

Pretzel's eyes brimmed with tears.

" You must promise then to return. I cannot bear it otherwise,"

"Martha my dear wife! You know that no Gratacian soul returns , that is not their way...those attractions tug at .."

"How would you know? And how can you let her go?"

Poppo's shoulders slumped as he took her arm, "This is the Gratacian way. We both know that ...We cannot talk like this any more. It is too painful to bear."

*

There was only two weeks to prepare, for Pretzel sensed that once the decision to leave is heralded by emotional farewells, the reasons for leaving turn into a whim that falls into thin air for the mind turns back on itself as self doubts grow. History had shown that many a Gratacian who had planned their departure, unpacked their bags again before carrying on as if nothing had happened. She knew she could not discuss her plans with anybody. There was too great a risk of their persuasive voices becoming too strong for her to resist.

Reza tightened her mouth when Pretzel knocked on her door with the request to sew multi- coloured padded pyjamas and spent the next days sewing and biting her tongue until the last buttons were in place.

"Planning to camp up with the goatherds with your Poppo, Eh?"

"You can say that."

Pretzel decided the best day to depart would be while the Lake Fest was in full progress, for no one would notice her heavy bundle being carried down the hill. People would assume it was simply her secret costume for the parade which was packed out of sight.

"Some Festival," Drako lamented, "My sister leaving me forever on that same day."

"No word of it, Drako." Poppo replied.

Martha and Poppo continued their daily grape picking into late evening to avoid the villagers' questionings if they were to sense their unhappiness. They were not seen at the Square for the evenings' festivities and were not missed, as they were known to be hard at work this time of year. Meanwhile, the two weeks seemed an eternity for Pretzel, as she and Drako continued with their schooling until the day before the Festival. Romela and Dashika walked with Pretzel up the hill, discussing excitedly the visiting musicians from Sharook. Pretzel had to bite her tongue, knowing her friends would never forgive her for simply disappearing without a goodbye. She hoped a day might come when they would both understand.

"I think Pretzel is up to something," Romela said later, "She keeps going quiet."

Dashika flicked her yellow plait to one side, "She is too proud now with her gown. She doesn't want to be seen with us."

"She might be planning a surprise item and keeping it to herself."

"That's more like her. She does that."

*

As soon as school was out, Drako wandered round the town centre, and when he saw his friends in the café, their faces reflecting the pinkness of the newly painted interior and excitedly chatting about the Springfest, he made a quick excuse to leave them. He wandered past the red stone walls of the "Lodge of the Ancients" and looked through the window to see that the madrigal singers were rehearsing. Normally he would have stayed outside and watched them but this time he continued down the stone steps that led into the catacombs. If he had lost points for his basketball team, if he had lost an argument with his father who had as good a memory as he was strong, if he had lost an arm wrestling match, particularly with Ricardo who seemed too puny to win at anything, or if he was simply feeling black for no obvious reason, this was the place he went. He sat on the low square monument of his ancestors where the names had been carved in for eternity and felt sick at the thought that not only was he losing his sister, but her name would never be there amongst them. He sat for a moment allowing his tears to fall until he heard a whimper. He peered into the blackness and realized that a young possum dog had fallen through a grille. He reached down and lifted it out as it gave a yelp and carried it up the steps into the light. He laid it down to remove the moss particles from its body and carried it back to the Square to give it water from the fountain. He soon discovered it could not stand as a back leg was broken. An old man sitting on the bench woke from his reverie to watch as Drako nestled the dog in his jacket before returning home. He manufactured a splint from a mala-koberry branch and was thrilled to see it had revived sufficiently to lap up warm goat's milk. He cleaned and dried the dog before burying his face in the red fur.

"You can comfort me when Pretz is gone."

Pretzel came out from her bedroom.

"You're not allowed to take them unless I'm …I 'm not dead yet!" then noticed the splint.

"The elders might let you keep him after he heals when they hear I have left for good. But I am not going to die, Drako."

"It is the same, Pretz."

She touched his suntanned nose with the tip of her fingers.

"My little brother, you must be brave."
"I will call my dog P.D. Short for Possum Dog,"
"Or Pretzel Dubajka."
They both laughed and hugged each other.
"He will keep you warm these nights."

*

Next morning Marthamum woke to find Pretzel packing her padded pyjamas into her cocoon sac and she felt faint. There was nothing further she could do or say. She went back to loading up her jars of marmalade, which became an orange blur in front of her.

The whole town was abuzz. Carts were piled with drinks and freshly baked bread rolls before being rumbled down the hill. It was not long before tents sprouted up displaying brightly coloured tassels flying from their tops. Hordes of children practiced walking on stilts, following behind old Devko who was loaded up with bundles of masks that grinned from his back.

Reza glanced over the wall and watched curiously as Pretzel forced handfuls of sultanas and dried apricots into every corner possible of her sac, but chose to say nothing.

The drummers began practicing for the evening's dance, the sound echoing round the cliffs. Youngster's heads appeared moving above the tents as the stilt competition was well in progress amidst shouts of encouragement.

Marthamum glanced at Pretzel's bundle.

"So you really mean it then?"

"Yes, Marthamum I really mean it. I am leaving tonight. I know none of you wanted to believe me."

"This village! Look at all this! Where could you find another to compare...... And your friends..."

"Please listen to me, Marthamum. It is not easy for me also, but tonight is the night I disappear. I did warn you of that and I cannot bear it either. "

"Then why, daughter, why?"

"Marthamum! One day you might understand. You must trust me. That is all I ask."

"We are leading you away. There is no turning back. We will lead you underneath the cliffs. "

Pretzel put her arm round her mother.

"I will find my way through… they are already leading me away. It is too late to change anything."

"But daughter. I have been happy here all my life, with your Poppo. We ask for nothing. You have become discontented and I feel helpless to stop you."

"You may never understand. I realize that now, but please try to, Marthamum. Oh please don't cry. "

"And what about Drako?"

Drako came to the door.

"I will be alright Marthamum. I have my possum dog now."

Pretzel laughed, "See! He is comforted already."

"I wish I could find comfort."

"You have Poppo."

Marthamum threw on her cream gown but her heart was not in to the usual preparations. She barely noticed Poppo's and Drako's embroidered shirts with their black shiny boots. She would have normally teased Poppo for the way he walked in them but not on this day.

They walked down the hill together pushing their cart stacked with Marthamum's jars alongside Pretzel's cocoon sac.

Shrill flutes drowned out any further conversation. Pretzel visited the stalls, gathering up further supplies of cheese rounds and grape jelly.

"Your parents will like those treats," shouted Hamisha, helping Pretzel place them in her sac.

Pretzel nodded. She was relieved that the loudness of the music prevented any further explanation. An aroma of coffee and shiskebabs came from the next tent.

"How I will miss that," she muttered.

She looked up the village perched on the cliff now white in afternoon sun. She wanted to drink in this image and keep it in her mind forever as she watched until she felt no longer part of it.

"I am a stranger now."

She rejoined her parents. Poppo could barely look at her. They sat together until dark and Drako joined them munching on berry tart. His sticky fingers touched her face and then he was gone again. When the dancing commenced, Poppo led Pretzel out onto the grass. She felt his thin strong bones as he held her spinning round and round until the music stopped.

"When the next dance comes it is a mixer and no one will notice me leaving, Poppo."

The flutes started up again, while the drummers came into the circle to lead the dance.

"No hugs. I cannot bear it."

She disappeared into the darkness.

*

*

CHAPTER 3   THE WINGFLITS

Lake Grataco shimmered softly in the moonlight. As the children's squeals and the sounds of accordions faded, the croaking of frogs became more apparent as Pretzel made her away along the edge. She turned from time to time to look back at the twinkling lights and gave a sigh of relief at not having to explain her self anymore. At last she was free. She could no longer bear another day of seeing the tears in Marthamum's eyes and the suppressed quivering of her lip, feeling the cruelest daughter in all of Grataco.

By the time she reached the far shore of the lake the moon had begun to set behind the cliffs and the sky became pockmarked with stars. She sat by the edge looking at their reflections. The night seemed endless as Pretzel began to imagine the monumental effect she would have on the entire village next morning. If she crept back home now before anyone noticed her gone, it would be a simple matter. She could carry on just as before. As she munched on her grandmother's, oatcakes she realized she will never see the old woman again and felt tinges of shame that she could not farewell her. She then wondered about her grandfather and Poppo's mixed reaction. It now began to make sense. This did not help her guilt and her misgivings continued until dawn appeared and her spirit flags revealed themselves.

"The path is before you now. Follow it and you will find what you must know…"

She immediately felt stronger of heart. The morning light turned the lake a milky blue, speared by the black and brown of the ducks and their new offspring strung out behind them. She was in no hurry to get up from the grassy bank and sat watching their antics until she was interrupted by a whirring of wings. She looked up with alarm at a funnel of black coming towards her and as the sound of flapping increased, a tower of birds reached up into what seemed infinity before dispersing and landing along the shore. Soon the lake was covered in a blanket of black feathers interspersed with their yellow beaks. Whenever they darted above her Pretzel caught flashes of bright green beneath their wings. Never in Grataco had she seen birds like these. They took their time to settle and perched on the grass around her, twittering. She thought of throwing pieces of her oatcakes to them, but for the necessity of hanging onto every morsel.

"Whippoo, whippoo."

"Sorry. I can't feed you now. I have to keep it all to myself. My humble apologies," laughed Pretzel.

The birds bobbed their heads from side to side, revealing a crimson band around their necks.

"It's nice to have company. I was feeling so alone."

"We too. We too."

Pretzel laughed for it sounded as if they were talking her language, so she responded, "Me too, me too."

"Whippoo,whippoo."

"How do how do," Pretzel replied, enjoying the fun and wishing she could share this with Drako. "I think you are talking to me."

"We are we are."

"Then who are you?"

"Whippoo, whippoo. You can't go back now."

Pretzel was dumbfounded. She looked around her to see if someone had crept up and was mocking her.

"Who's talking to me now? Or have I gone crazy already!"

"We are the wingflits."

Pretzel looked at them all in surprise. "You birds talk?"

"We are the wingflits," they repeated in unison, "We will take you to the...."

"I'm Sorro," interrupted one of the birds, flapping its wings ostentatiously before pirouetting on one claw.

"And I'm Batwin."

"I'm Tachymus."

"And I'm Roland."

"And I'm...."

"You mean you all have names! There are trillions of you!"

The birds became quiet and looked at her expectantly.

"Well. What now!"

Pretzel was glad there was no one around, for she would have been gently led back into Grataco, and taken to the village 'healer of lost minds.'

The birds continued to observe her silently.

"What's the matter? Oh, sorry. My name is Pretzel."

"Manners, my girl," twittered Sorro as he darted around her.

"Put a beak in it, Sorro," chirped Batwin.

"Pipe down the pair of you," exclaimed Tachymus.

"You are a mob of twits!" blurted out Pretzel, instantly embarrassed at her weak joke as the wingflits muttered to each other about having heard this one before.

They all looked at her condescendingly.

"I am sorry. I didn't mean to be rude. It was just a joke."

"You said you were taking me to where?"

"To farewell the lake."

"How do I do that?"

Tachymus nodded his head as a bird with an unusual beak landed in front of her.

"You pick up this stone, hold it above your head and you throw it into the center of the lake. Then you say, "I leave the lake for unknown lands and lead me to the…"

"Shhh, Batwin" interrupted Tachymus, "It is better not to mention the…"

"Lead me to the what?" inquired Pretzel, looking from one bird to other in disbelief.

"Yes, exactly!"

"She said 'what'. Not the Wattoo."

"What is the Wattoo?"

"What what what," chirped Sorro, flying and tumbling over his tail feathers.

"We will say no more," Tachymus added solemnly. "But you must farewell the lake, properly."

"Then please show me what I must do."

Batwin held an object in his beak, which flashed in the sunlight. He placed it on the sand in front of Pretzel.

"A topaz from Tarzon! Where did you find this?"

She picked it up and gazed into its center which displayed swirling colours of brilliant reds and gold. She had seen the occasional one in Grataco set in brooches of the old women. They had been mined many years ago from the mountains of Northern Tarzon. Small broken ones were occasionally seen amongst the rubble left behind. But the completely oval or oblong shaped jewels were dug from tunnels far underground. The miners risked their lives, and withstood freezing conditions to collect them. These men were held in high regard, for it meant wealth to the inhabitants. There were stories of their being smuggled over the pinnacles of the Upper Tarzon, but that rarely happened as a miner caught smuggling would be banished forever.

"We chose this from the highest cave. Look at Batwin's beak."

Pretzel had already noticed Batwin's beak. It was worn down to a dome shape and ingrained with black dirt. She tried to picture this tiny bird flying into the cold and oppressive darkness, grinding away at the hard rock that enclosed it, and then picking it out intact.

"Why go to this trouble. What do birds need with a precious stone like this?"

She stared into it again, admiring the flickers of red like a fire with sparks of gold in constant movement.

"To throw into the lake."

"You mean you go to all this trouble just to throw it away?"

"No more questions. Just chuck it," interrupted Batwin.

"Chuck! Chuck! Chuck!" the rest twittered.

Pretzel held it in her hand but could not let it go.

"You must."

"Must must must," was the refrain as Pretzel could see there was no use arguing, and in any case, she surmised, it was not hers in the first place, so reluctantly threw it underarm. She knew she was never the best at throwing things so watched it land miserably on the shore. The lake became a mass of foam which released three snakes slithering towards her.

"Pick it up and throw it properly," ordered Tachymus as by this time the rest of the wingflits were occupying the pines, well out of danger.

"Imagine it is cricket. Bowl if you must."

Pretzel bowled as quickly as she could with one eye on the nearest snake. This time the stone skimmed across the water but hit a rock and back it returned to land at her feet. To her relief the snakes retreated back into the water, but this time she was surrounded by the angriest, slimiest and greenest toads of all of the district of Grataco.

"Croquet or cricket or croak it!" the wingflits called from the trees.

"Get it in the center or they will ooze you with their poisonous yellow from their glum and miserable glands and…" Batwin was lost for words as the toads hopped, stank and surrounded Pretzel.

"I need you to help me!" Pretzel cried, not knowing whether to stay still or run for cover.

Sorro quickly flew down and picked up the stone in his beak. He washed it before depositing it in front of Pretzel. He was very wet and looked as sorrowful as a small bird could.

"Get it in the thenthre this time, "Sorro lisped spraying water from his beak, "We have no time to wasthe."

Pretzel hurled it for the third time. It was a perfect landing, giving one small splash before disappearing into the deep. The toads hopped away grumbling and clicketting into some rock pools, their eyes only visible regarding her with a fixed stare.

This time the lake became very still. The reflections from the pines gradually disappeared and in their place was a changing array of colours. The more Pretzel gazed, the deeper the colours became until they were as black as a moonless midnight. Then there were star shapes, strange creeping things, followed by a deep pit of intense blue. Pretzel could have stayed forever looking into it. She became aware of her flags which waved in front of her as the pit lightened in colour and the reflection from the pine trees returned.

Pretzel felt a thrill of excitement up and down her spine, knowing now she would never turn back.

"Don't look behind you now. Follow us."
The cloud of wingflits led her into the morning sun.

*

The sun rose onto the last revelers by the lake. Marthamum and Poppo, who had drunk too many carafes of wine in attempt to damp down the loss of Pretzel, had staggered home well before the celebrations had ended while Drako stayed up throughout the night resisting the urge to race after his sister.

Next morning Drako needed to be alone to avoid the inevitable questions from his friends, so made his way along the top of the cliff followed by his now faithful possum dog. As he continued along the southern edge, he noticed a haze above the lake. There were often small storms this time of year so he figured it must be a small willy- willy, but all the same felt a shiver down his spine. He leant over the edge in the vain hope that his sister was returning along the track below and waving up to him, but all he could see were two donkeys standing together looking forlorn.

He continued sadly along the cliff edge until her reached the part where it was no longer safe as the edges were beginning to crumble away. He was about to turn back but he noticed something glinting and wondered if the heavy rains had eroded away some harder quartz. He smoothed away the soil and to his surprise found a dog collar buried there. He scraped off the mud and proceeded to spit on it and rub it clean, where to his amazement he could see there were six topaz all of different sizes and shapes inlaid into the leather. He wondered if it had once belonged to a Tarzonian many years ago for no Gratacian would waste these precious gems on a dog collar. On returning home, he oiled the leather and polished up the stones.

He heard his parents arriving at the back gate and was about to call out to them but something stopped him. This will be his secret. He will keep it buried there in P.D.'s long fur as a talisman to give him hope that one day his sister might return. At night he would be able to lift up the fur and watch their redness glinting in the moonlight.

CHAPTER 4   THE HETZENBABEL

The wingflits surrounded Pretzel, twittering loudly as she made her way towards the far end of the lake. The chalets were deserted due to the Midsummer Fest but soon would be ringing with children's voices. She peered through a window to see soft mattresses and fluffy pillows wondering if she would ever find such comfort again. When she looked back at Grataco, the cliff homes looked bright and clear against the blue sky. She felt another surge of excitement knowing that this well used stone path which she had danced along as a child will come to a sudden halt. Memories flooded in of Marthamum and Poppo quickly turning around as if they had been burnt with a hot poker. She had not questioned them then; her world which ceased at this point, but now she was about to pass the cairn of stones which marked the point of no return. Beyond it lay a small grey shoe, no doubt left behind by a group of picnickers too afraid to retrieve it for their child.

Tachymus urged her past, darting and diving around her as Roland flew above leading the way. Pretzel's spirit flags gave a joyful whoop as she passed the cairn, but when she turned to look back at the lake, now a flat blue pencil, she suddenly felt such a heaviness in her legs she threw herself on the ground.

"You can't stop here. The wilderness awaits you."

The flags frantically waved above while Sorro made vain attempts to cheer her up by trying to balance on one wing, toppling over with his clawed feet in the air, but she was not in a laughing mood. The magnitude of what she had just done overwhelmed her as she thought of Marthamum placing her black headdress on and following Poppo sadly up the hill. She imagined she had heard a call, followed by the bleating of goats but shook away the images as she picked herself up and started off again, trying not to heed her misgivings. She brushed past a cluster of spiked plants that pierced her arms and made them bleed. The pack soon began to feel heavier as with each step, the jars of grape jam knocked against her shoulder blades but Pretzel felt she could not be seen to complain too much in front of her new friends so tried as best she could to put on a brave face.

The ground gradually became sandier. Small trees sprouted branches, giving her the occasional blotch of shade. From time to time she stopped to rest and to drink from her metal bottle while the wingflits perched on the branches above or hopped around her on the hot sand. She berated herself many times for leaving in the height of summer until she reminded herself her flags had chosen this time to call her. At times she berated herself for not having resisted the call of her flags, but it was too late. Now she had passed the cairn, she had to trust them.

"Where do we find water, Tachymus?" she asked eventually, trying her hardest to sound in control.

"We will find it. You will see."

As far as Pretzel could see, there was no lake or river in sight, and by late afternoon she was worried. She put her pack down.

"Please, Tachymus. Show me where water is, or else I may have to go back regardless."

"Cant go. Cant go," chimed the wingflits.

"Then where is the water as you promised?"

Roland circled an area that to Pretzel looked exactly like the terrain she had been walking on, and only then she noticed his elongated beak pointing downwards to a spot on the sand. The rest began to dig using their beaks and claws, throwing up sand all around them and half burying Sorro who kept getting in the way until he flapped off to find a perch as the wingflits continued to dig until they disappeared below the surface. At last the sand became moist and a pool of muddy water appeared in the depths of the hole.

"Fill your bottle first," suggested Tachymus.

The wingflits waited for her and then began to drink and bathe joined by Sorro who, Pretzel was to discover, always took the longest. This was followed by his cheerful somersaults into the fine sand which stuck to his wings. This was then an excuse to repeat the exercise. Pretzel felt in better spirits, and laughed at his antics. She could see he would be the one to cheer her up when she felt afraid.

When it was time to continue on the afternoon sun began to lose its warmth and Pretzel looked for shelter from the night's chill wind. She stopped by some overhanging rock and laid out her cocoon sac, munching on her bread and jam as the wingflits surveyed her curiously.

"Sorry to eat in front of you."

She needn't have worried, for at dusk billions of flying insects surrounded them. She could see why they called themselves the wingflits, as they darted hither and thither, the green under their wings flashing in the evening light. She now felt an extreme calm as she rested her back on the warm rock and remained awake to watch the full moon rise, and with it the shadows of the rocks and trees appearing stark as in daylight. Throughout the night she heard the occasional squawk as the birds nudged each other for space. Pretzel pulled the sac to her chin and drifted off into sleep as the flags swayed above her.

As soon as the sun's rays warmed her face, Pretzel crawled out and examined her collection of dried fruit. She had enough to last for several weeks. Now that the water incident was past, she felt more confident that between the wingflits and her flags, she would manage but could not help wondering what might have happened if the wingflits had not appeared. She imagined that if she was to return to Grataco, relating how easy her journey so far had been, would they believe her? Talking birds that helped her find water? But then she remembered, 'Of course there will be no such greeting. I am lost to them now.'

For many days the group continued southward beneath the cliffs. The wingflits rarely left her side, particularly Sorro, who flitted close to her feet. Roland was more wary and kept his distance, flying on ahead and only returning to report of any dangers.

"Eagles," Tachymus explained.

After more days they came across tall trees with the occasional cluster of berries. Pretzel sampled one cautiously. It had a soft yellow centre which tasted like a citrus flavoured date, so picked all she could find to stuff into her sac. She began to feel more energetic as she strode beneath the cliff edge which each day felt was becoming like an old friend protecting her from the afternoon sun.

Many mornings later, Batwin stood in front of her, waiting till she had stretched and rolled up her sac for another long walk before the sun reached its peak.

"We will have to pass the........."

Tachymus interrupted him.

"Don't tell her. Not yet. No need to terrify the girl."

"What are you two chirping about?"

"That it is time for your breakfast."

Pretzel stared at the two of them, puzzled at their concern about her mealtimes, but was loathe to argue so ate more of her dates until the wingflits were content to continue on. She started to sing as she walked and immediately they responded by twittering in unison. Pretzel stopped her singing and listened spellbound. From then on the days seemed shorter as they entertained each other in this manner.

But one morning Batwin greeted her again.

"Today we have to pass the…"

"I said before, don't tell the girl," interrupted Tachymus.

Pretzel remained puzzled as she walked on until suddenly the wingflits halted at a massive boulder which leant out over their path. Roland flew down.

"It's awake!"

"What! Who?" Pretzel asked, looking round her.

"No noise. Not a sound."

"What on earth…"

"Just do as I say."

Pretzel looked at her boots that squeaked with each step.

"Take them off!"

She untied her shoelaces and yanked off her boots as she pointed to the sharp pebbles ahead.

"They will crunch when I walk on them." she whispered.

"Watch."

At once the wingflits perched in a line and spread out their tail feathers.

"Walk on them."

"But I will crush…"

"Their feathers are sturdy. Walk. Not a sound now."

Pretzel separated her pots of jam with clothing to muffle the clunks, and carrying her shoes in her hand, trod carefully along the wing tips. As soon as she arrived at the end of the row of birds they replaced themselves further along the track. At times she came to a sandy patch where they could all rest before continuing on. When they were almost past this massive rock Pretzel looked up to see a deep slit halfway up its side inside which a green shapeless mass glinted, producing a stench of rotting mice and bats.

"Ugh!" cried Pretzel, overpowered by the smell, then slapped her hand over her mouth as the shape suddenly became alive, reaching a sticky tentacle towards her.

"You've done it now!" Batwin exclaimed.

The finger like projection continued to swell. On the end of it was a purple claw from which dripped green fluid. The wingflits flapped around her, attempting to distract the creature until at last she was beyond its reach. She turned with relief only to find the claw receding into the slit with clumps of wingflits still attached. Particles of feathers wafted down to the sand which was spattered with drops of blood. The smell faded as the group silently watched from a safe distance until Tachymus eventually commented gravely.

"The Hetzenbabel has grown enormous since last spring."

Pretzel was dry retching.

"Why didn't you warn me?"

"You wouldn't have come. Simply that."

Her shock turned to anger.

"How could you put all of yourselves at risk on my account? You could have flown off. Those poor little birds....."

"It was the only way,"

"You are here aren't you?" Roland added.

"But your little mates..."

Tachymus explained as if to a youngster who knew nothing.

"We are food also, edible to others. It is our lot in life. Look at those eagles."

Above them, black shapes soared above the cliff. Pretzel felt immediately humbled by these gallant wingflits that accepted such risks and loss of life as normal .

"Tell me about that... thing."

"The Hetzenbabel was an ordinary snake many years past. It fed on mice, rabbits, us, the usual prey. But then it found food was so abundant, it could strike at will without having to leave its cave within the rock. It grew longer and plumper until one day it found it had grown too large to leave the entrance and it was trapped for ever. In order to survive it grew that extra appendage. First its prey could scratch, bite, or peck to escape, so it cleverly devised this sticky substance. Here. Some is still stuck to your back."

Several birds began to peck gently at Pretzel's clothes, removing the particles. She shuddered. No longer did her grape jelly seem palatable.

"Let's get out of this place"

Pretzel trekked on until the sun hovered over the cliff casting long shadows. As the birds were quiet since their encounter with the Hetzenbabel, Pretzel felt it an imposition to ask them more questions. At last they reached a small spring from which bubbled up cool water. Pretzel splashed her face as the wingflits bathed spraying her with the cool particles.

Eventually Roland spoke.

"We must reach the top of the cliff before nightfall as there are no more trees to protect us."

"We lead you into the desert. We must lead you away from the cliffs."

She remembered her flags appearing in her dreams and pointed east.

"I must go the other way."

Tachymus flew down at her feet.

"Now listen, dear human girl. We are trying to explain to you we must go up as we cannot remain here overnight."

"Up up up," added Sorro, as he chirped around her.

Pretzel saw footholds in the rock. It would be an easy climb and in no way wished to part with her friends.

"The winged things are leading me up the steep trail. Flags go away!"

Pretzel began to follow the birds but she was soon accosted by her flags that were in frenzy.

"The desert awaits you. Follow us. You must follow!"

From half way up the cliff when she studied the sand below she could make out a dust covered path leading directly away from the cliff. It was now obvious what she must do.

"I am sorry wingflits. I must return to the spring and wait for tomorrow."

The birds surrounded her.

"We cannot go with you." Tachymus explained.

"I do understand that, Tachymus, for there is no shelter."

"You're on your own, then." Batwin remarked, fluffing up his feathers.

"You'll be sorry." added Sorro, who was dipping and diving in an attempt to block her downward climb.

"Oh, Sorro. How I will miss you."

"Do not stand on the yellow." Roland warned.

"Time to bid farewell." announced Tachymus.

One by one the wingflits flew by Pretzel's face, fluttering their wings softly onto her cheek. She recalled the 'butterfly' kisses she had received from Poppo before bedding down for the night. Tears rolled down her face which mingled with the downy feathers of each bird as wing by wing they fluttered their goodbyes. In the purple twilight she could make out tiny specks disappearing into the trees above.

"They saved my life. Now they are gone. I had no time to thank them all properly or anything."

Pretzel scrambled her way back to the spring and buried her face in a tuft of grass until the wind blew chill down her neck. She unrolled her cocoon sac and crawled in, clutching her pillow, her whole body shaking. The night seemed endless as distant howls sent tingles down her spine. Her stomach ached with longing for her small friends. There was not even a moon to cheer her, not until the early hours of the morning when it rose over the plain, making the clumps of rock appear alive and she thought she could see snakes slithering past her.

When she eventually slept she dreamt of her brother who lay nestling his nose into the fur of his possum dog. He was fingering a leather collar, feeling cool shapes until the morning light cast them in a reddish glow.

CHAPTER 5   THE SHIMMERS

Shards of light played across Pretzel's closed lids. She felt a soft breeze on her cheeks which had replaced the chill night wind, as she lay there aware of the comforting closeness of the cliffs which would soon be gone, replaced by the flatness of the desert and the open skies stretching for ever. When she crawled out, she looked up in the hope of seeing her winged friends, but there was not a speck in the sky. She wondered if they may be watching her from the safety of the trees. She crouched by the spring to splash her face and started to wonder if this had all been a dream. However, a remnant of the green substance on her jacket convinced her that the purple claw was not a nightmare. She scraped the particle off with a stick in case any poison remained.

"Follow us. We are leading you towards the sun."

She looked up at her flags that danced in the golden light as if they had not a care in the world, and dutifully filled her bottles before starting off towards the orange ball on the horizon. The desert pebbles glistened in the early light and fine red dust flew around her ankles as she walked. She passed patches of tiny pink flowers which became sparser, before disappearing altogether. After some hours she turned to look back at the cliffs, again doubting her good sense, but the flags continued to wave her eastward. When the sun was at its highest, she shaded herself under her sac, glad that it would soon be autumn with its promise of cooler days and hope of rain. When night came, the silence was so immense she could hear the beating of her heart.

The next day, after trekking without finding food or water, Pretzel began to worry.

"I should have followed the wingflits after all," she muttered, but her flags continue to wave above her.

"Keep walking straight ahead and we will not abandon you."

"And if there is no water? I will die and it will be your fault! Show me that I can survive out here, or else I will never listen to you again."

She then laughed in spite of her misgivings.

"That is silly. If I didn't survive I wouldn't be listening to them anyway!" which was responded with what sounded like a silvery chuckle from the nearest flag.

She walked on until twilight when a mist came down. She could make out dark shapes in front of her and decided to stop, remembering the Hetzenbabel, but at first light she discovered they were simply clusters of deep green cacti which reached way above her height. Each plant was twisted into a unique shape as if in a strange sculpture exhibition. She stuck her knife into one and out seeped a pinkish fluid. She put some on her finger to taste. It was sour. She waited to see if there was any ill effect before slicing more of the stems, gathering courage to suck them. It was refreshing. The flesh had the consistency of cucumber and satisfied her appetite.

"It's not a huge repertoire at this café but will have to make do," she laughed, relieved that she could really survive out here and looked up at her flags.

"I should have trusted you."

She collected as many as she could. They weighed her down and squelched together as she walked. Now that the cacti appeared at frequent intervals, she felt confident to continue on but another day went past before the monotony began to bother

her. Her flags were not exactly chatty, and she missed badly the company of the wingflits.

After a few more days of trekking, there had been little change in the landscape bar the occasional wispy cloud, so she was gratified when a rock appeared in the distance. When at last she reached it, she walked round its base, checking it thoroughly for slits or holes that could harbour another Hetzenbabel like creature before scrambling up to survey the view. The desert shimmered before her as always, becoming a haze on the horizon with still no end in sight. She stood on the top, straining her eyes for more rocks in the distance when she felt a sharp sting. A huge red ant as large as a Grataco garden beetle was attached to her sock, followed by a carpet of them scuttling up the rock toward her. She beat at them with her sac which had little effect, but in the process, a cactus stalk fell out and landed amongst them. The ants scattered to demolish the flesh, allowing her to climb back down and at a safe distance, examined her foot which began to swell. How she missed Marthamum's soothing balm as tears ran down her cheeks.

She looked up at her flags hoping for a word of compassion but they seemed preoccupied, forming a huddle before waving her on again.

She dragged herself up and limped eastward, beginning to have visions of the little stream bubbling through Grataco, of the grass clad mountains and of the old folk sitting in chairs gossiping out their days. Now Marthamum would be bottling her apricots, or turning them into jam or chutney. She felt twinges of guilt as her parents would be clinging to each other these long nights. She had to keep reminding herself that she had in an odd way a blessing from her father in the way he had hushed up Marthamum, and that she must now keep going until she arrives at... where? What she feared most was the image of herself wandering off into the desert with her arms in front of her, eyes glazed. Each time she thought of that, the fear of losing her mind caused her to jump up and trudge on pretending to herself she was on her way toward a known destination.

There were many long days of trudging, checking on her foot each day. It had turned purplish colour but no longer hurt. The nights had a piercing chill that went straight through her cocoon sac. It seemed an eternity until the sun appeared with its first pale warmth before the intense midday heat. She would then try to cover her head but her eyes felt dry and painful if the wind blew and her hands started to look brown and crusted like Marthamum's. She was far away from their reprimands. A young girl must keep her hands white, smooth and supple. Pretzel again felt that thrill of freedom as she looked at them and wondered how her face would appear… like old grandmother Varsla's?

"I don't care. I just don't care," she called to her flags, skipping along behind them, "And I am not going out of my mind after all."

She remained in great spirits as she woke each morning until one day she thought she was sure she could hear a waterfall in the distance. She thought perhaps her mind was starting to play tricks after all as she continued to walk with nothing that looked like a riverbed and no rocks to suggest a hidden waterfall. But the rushing sound gradually became louder until it became deafening. She approached the sound until she reached a collection of vast pools, each a brilliant colour. There was a narrow path of sand that she could step on between them as they continued their loud swishing and gurgling to each side of her. There were pools of startling turquoise, a deepest red and purple resembling the colours of Reza's silks.

She stood mesmerized like a child that is drawn in to something both sinister and exciting. She threw a cactus stalk into the red pool watching it disappear into the depths becoming a speck as it sunk and she shivered at the thought what would happen if she was to fall in. She steadied herself as curiosity got the better of her, throwing another at a large purple pool. The edges rolled up and devoured the stalk as if alive. There was a blue oblong shaped pool that gave a hiss as the fruit was thrown back at her, covering her in a fine blue spray which pricked her skin like a myriad of fine needles.

"The blue doesn't fancy cactus fruit!" she called to her flags.

"No one has spoken of these before," she said to herself with amazement until she reminded herself that no one has ever returned to relate what they had found and looked up again at her flags for comfort.

She walked along, happily throwing particles of the stems into the pools until at last there appeared a square of yellow sand on which she could sit and stretch out. She did not see the flags desperately swiping at the air in front of her until it was too late. To her horror it was not as she thought. Instead a thick bog held her in a sucking grip and too late she realized what Roland's hurried warning had meant when he called, "Do not stand on the yellow."

She decided to try a swimming crawl towards the edge, but every time she extracted a limb it would be grabbed back again and her attempts at moving just made her sink in more into its cloying depths. There was nothing she could do but stay as still as possible. By nightfall the desert wind blew like icicles down her neck, but she dared not reach over to cover herself with her sac , so sat the night out in terror calling to her flags that remained above in ghostly apparition. By morning she was hungry, regretting she had thrown most of her cacti away but realized what remained in her sac was beyond her reach anyway.

"What use are you to me now, flags," she whimpered as they moved above her combing the sky as if they had all day and not a care in the world.

Pretzel knew it would not be long before she would die if she was to spend many more freezing nights here without food. Already she felt weakened and decided to see if she could roll her body on the top of the sand. At one moment she felt she could pull one leg out and then it gave way until just her head and shoulders were above the sand. It was no use. She knew she would not last now and thought of Grataco. She thought of her funeral that would never exist. She thought of her brother surpassing her in age as she withered into the faintest of memories. She thought of Poppo, the sad curious expression and then realized why he had never spoken of her grandfather. 'How many wanderers have met their fate here,' she thought. All this went through her mind as the hot sun warmed her head until the chill began and she could not bear the hunger pangs eating into her belly that felt cramped inside the bog making her want to vomit. Yet Pretzel surprised herself.

"I am still glad." she whispered, as her eyes stung with the realization of this. "I am still glad I left Grataco. I am still glad I followed my flags to my death. I am still glad I followed the wingflits. I am still glad I followed…..I followed ….me."

Pretzel closed her eyes and felt an immense peace despite her situation until the sun rose again to warm her face.

"I am no longer afraid to die alone," she whispered to herself. "I am not alone. I have the desert and my flags. I am not alone and I am going to die and it won't be long now for I can feel…"

Her thoughts were interrupted by the sound of a screech above the swish of the pools and the flapping of wings.

"Take the topaz quick."

She could see from the corner of her eye the domed beak of Batwin.

"My hands are stuck!"

"Take it in your mouth, try not to swallow it, and throw it in the bog."

Pretzel gripped the stone between her teeth as Batwin released it gently from his talon before flying away in haste. She then spat out the topaz onto the mud which gave a sucking sound and the stone instantly vanished. Slowly Pretzel was able to extricate her self together with her sac that was sticky with mud. She searched for Batwin in the sky but there was no sign of him. She was removing the mud from her boots in readiness to continue along the path and heard a splat and in front of her landed a pile of mud. She was about to run for her life, but when she saw the glint of red protruding out of it she quickly extracted it and ran on until the desert returned as before and the sounds of rushing water fading into the usual hush of wind.

As soon as she felt safe to rest, she scraped the remaining mud from her sac which smelt of dead animals. She then examined the stone which she recognized as a topaz the way it shone in the bright afternoon light and sobbed with relief and exhaustion. But it was time to move on towards a group of cacti before night fell and she devoured the flesh hungrily. She thought of the stone she had thrown into Lake Grataco and her reluctance to part with it until the wingflits had urged her.

"I will never ever part with this stone. My beloved Batwin! It will remind me of my beloved wingflits and how you saved my life."

She suddenly noticed her thought flags that were hovering above her.

"And what use were my flags! Was this some kind of a joke? Why didn't you warn me?"

"See what you have now discovered."

She could not get any further explanation from them as she felt for the stone in her pocket. In silence her flags led her on again until her shadow lengthened before her. She was soon aware how exhausted she was now that the danger had passed but she was intoxicated with relief at escaping such a suffocating death. She dug herself a hollow in the sand as she had done so many times before and this time felt no longer daunted by the long night. She lay there in her sac staring up at the stars feeling they were also becoming her friends before they faded into blackness of sleep.

*

Drako had been up with the goatherds all day, moving them down to more lush pastures, before returning home to eat thick creamy potato soup with Marthamum and Poppo. They were quieter these nights which saddened him. He crawled into bed and reached out to stroke his possum dog and to feel along the collar for the stones, but felt a dip and sat up to turn the light on. There were only five stones, and when he searched the floor the only thing he found was one green feather.

CHAPTER 6   THE SARADENS.

Pretzel woke and buried herself deeper into the soft sand, for despite Reza's padded pyjamas, her feet were numb and her back felt as if licked by merciless tongues. She welcomed dawn at last when the wind died down and she could crawl out and stamp her feet. She gathered up more supplies of cactus stalks before trudging on, making the most of the morning's coolness.

The desert haze lifted, revealing white specks in the distance. Pretzel quickened her pace in an attempt to reach them but they were further away than she thought. She spent another freezing night before jumping up at first light, and by late afternoon they had materialized into tall towers, their whiteness dazzling in the bright sunlight. As she came nearer she could see they were contained within a high wall that stretched away to the south and when at last she reached them she could see there were stairs spiraling up their sides and at frequent intervals were oblong shaped windows like a children's drawing. The wall loomed above her as she approached a massive gate .A distinct aroma of onions and barbecued meat wafted down reminding Pretzel of what seemed a lifetime ago....carrots, dumplings, chunks of cheese, buttery dollops, water from a cool terracotta urn being poured into stone cups, and vats of red wine. Her flags waved frantically.

"Follow the path that leads you to the South. The River Banzoor awaits you."

Pretzel refused to take heed. Her stomach was rumbling badly so she shrugged them off and knocked on the gate which gave a metallic boom. When she peered through the keyhole, she could make out a group of people standing on the other side.

"Excuse me."

No one heard her. She found a rock and banged on the gate loudly. One of the men looked up in surprise. He walked to the gate and peered through while Pretzel blocked her ears to keep out the incessant calling from her flags.

"Please can you let me in. I have been on a long journey across the desert. I would appreciate it if I could buy something to eat."

He gave a guffaw and unlocked the gate which closed with a clang behind her and when she looked around it was hard to make it out from the rest of the wall. This alarmed her but the smell of pork was too tantalizing for her to care. She looked around at the group. They were mostly short and with square build, decked out in long brightly coloured cardigans from which protruded wooden clogs. When they frequently burst into laughter it was accompanied by a quaint toe tapping dance.

Another cluster of men stopped mid conversation to survey the tall girl who had materialized out of nowhere. Eventually one came over and greeted her. The top of his head reached her breastbone. He took her hand and helped her up the grassy embankment. Pretzel noted the grass was similar to the fields of Grataco except these leaf blades were shorter, broader and sprouting crimson flowers.

"Enchanting."

The man beamed at her.

"Please sit."

Pretzel sat awkwardly on the low seat offered to her, knees tucked up to her chest.

"You must be from the North. You are tall like them. My name is Tarod."

Pretzel turned to look back at the imposing walls.

"My name is Prêtzova, but call me Pretzel. I hope you don't mind me intruding…"

"Ha. No one here remains a visitor," another man interrupted.

"Why not?" Pretzel asked in alarm.

"They like it here too much so they stay."

With that he rolled about the grass laughing uproariously. Pretzel was in no position to see the joke but smiled to be polite. He sat up and flicked his pigtail to one side, staring at her with green eyes that looked her up and down appraisingly.

"Why come all this way? You don't look like a spy?"

"No, I am not a spy. I would not know what a spy is meant to do. I was on my way to the other side of the desert and when I reached these magnificent towers and smelt your delicious food just like my Marthamum's….."

"You can eat at my house," Tarod interrupted quickly, "Follow me."

Pretzel glanced behind at the man with the pigtail who continued to gape with surprise, as she hurried behind Tarod, his steps quick despite the shortness of his legs. The path glistened with the same white stones that made up the towers. They passed a group of women, their faces soft and round with large green eyes. They quickly nudged each other and broke into wide smiles when they saw her. They were swathed in shawls that covered half their short bodies below which were wool skirts and similar quaint clogs that the men wore. They waved a greeting as their children clad in thick felt overalls, skipped behind her until they were called back. An old woman showed her toothless gums and waved with her handkerchief before blowing it loudly, much to the mirth of the other women.

"Valleka is giving you a welcome," they laughed.

"What a cheerful lot of people!" Pretzel exclaimed, puffing when she caught up to Tarod.

"Yep." Tarod replied, waiting patiently whenever she stopped to survey the gardens on each side. When the path continued up a steep incline, Pretzel could see the village square below displaying market stalls with dome shaped roofs from which hung variegated flags. She watched as a group of women filled their pots from the fountain before carrying them up the spiral staircases.

She glanced down at Tarod's face which was brown and lined no doubt from the dry desert wind and harsh sunlight. Now that they were away from curious eyes he appeared serious.

"Yes," he repeated tersely, "It appears a happy place to live."

He made no further comment as they ascended until they reached a landing where Tarod again allowed Pretzel to draw breath. She leaned on the balustrade looking down onto the walls with the desert stretching beyond.

"My people descended from a mix of Saraden and Tarzonian. I am ore Tarzonian in looks and Larrida is almost pure Saraden. That is why she is a little taller than I. We have lived in this city for centuries together now. There are still some pure Tarzonians whose offspring, the ones that escaped, live in the mountains to the far north."

"Where they mine the topaz?"

"Some still speak in the old language. You will hear the tongue clicking by the old folk."

"The topaz? They have been brought all this way?"

"So you also know of them. They were mined and brought here to trade as the Saraden emperor wanted them in exchange for this white rock that you see makes up most of our city. He instead captured them as slaves as they were of strong build and would be of good use to mine the Pradi. That is the name of this rock. He took from them all the topaz in order to turn this into a jeweled city. You will see the only remaining topaz inlaid high in the city bell where none can reach."

Pretzel felt for the topaz safely tucked in her pocket but decided it wiser to say nothing.

"What happened to all the jewels?"

"There was a revolt and a few of the slaves escaped with all but a few that were used for the bell. Some descendents hoped to travel north to find more but they would not have been trusted to return with them so it is too late. We now love our white Pradi that as you can see glows brilliantly when the sun strikes, so we continue to mine them."

"What happened to the Tarzonians that were left behind?"

"They continued to be forced into the mines. Because of their strength and muscular build they were sought after by the women. At first this was not acceptable until the emperor realized that their offspring would now be strong little Saradens and there would be no further revolt."

"Then why do you need such a high wall?"

"Eat with us, and I will explain more."

They climbed further until Tarod stopped at an arched doorway requiring Pretzel to duck her head as he led her in. The interior was dark and lit by candles. As Pretzel's eyes became accustomed, she could see that Tarod's face had relaxed but there was a resignation in his expression that she had not noticed before. Three plump boys sat playing a game with an assortment of stones with symbols carved into each one. They looked up as Pretzel and Tarod entered and quickly forced a smile before staring at her with their round eyes. A woman ladling soup looked with alarm at Pretzel. until Tarod indicated to her to get another bowl. Her face was also plump like her sons and her braided hair had flecks of grey similar to that of Marthamum. She wore a long turquoise jumper inlaid with flakes of what Pretzel guessed was the Pradi. Pretzel, who was now dizzy with hunger, gratefully followed the other's example and lifted her bowl to her lips slurping loudly.

It was not until the bowls were cleared away, that Tarod took his wife aside to explain the circumstances of Pretzel's arrival and that she was not spying on their behaviour. She reached out her hand.

"I am Larrida."

"I am Pretzel.. I am so glad I have come to this magnificent place, but I am just visiting here."

"Yes. I hear you say you were."

Pretzel noticed with unease that she deliberately used the past tense.

"These are our boys, Bedum, Tarodnik, and Gapsel. You are safe with us," she added, "You don't need to laugh here."

Pretzel gave an embarrassed chuckle at what seemed to her an odd kind of game.

"Shhh. We really can't stand the sound of it anymore."

Pretzel put her hand to her mouth.

"The poor girl is confused, Larrida." Tarod said, watching her discomfort, "Explain more to her."

"We must warn you. Things aren't what they seem. When you are out in the street you must look cheerful at all times, but you are safe in here."

Pretzel looked baffled.

"This is the city of smiling people." Tarod added with a grimace.

"Oh. How quaint!"

"No. Not if it is compulsory. It is not so easy..."

"But if you are as friendly as this isn't it easy?"

Pretzel was instantly ashamed of her insensitivity as the boys winced.

They sat together in silence again as the flatbread was passed around, each breaking off a piece. Pretzel noticed the fireplace built in the wall and the baskets of potatoes and beans by the door of the minute kitchen which could only contain one person at a time.

Eventually Pretzel felt it was time to question Tarod further.

"Why do they say you have to look happy all the time?"

"As I began to explain, when the Tarzon people arrived with their topaz, the Saradens captured them instead and took them as their slaves, keeping the topaz for themselves until they were stolen back. The remaining Tarzonians first missed their northern mountains so terribly that they were prepared to risk death in the desert on order to return. They sung of the mountains to their children and when they were silenced the stories were whispered down about their northern land. Then the emperor came up with a plan. If there were tall towers, the children would see them as mountains and have no wish to escape. The slaves built these towers over the years and are still being erected to this day using chips of the Pradi as inlay."

"And the rules about being happy?"

"Well, the slaves worked out if they seemed happy in their work, the Saradens may relax and be less vigilant. But in time the Saraden's offspring felt they now belonged. There was no further talk of the mountains anymore but the word was passed around to pretend to be happy in their work at all times. Then as more time passed, the city leader Banituk [we don't call them emperors anymore as we are meant to be more democratic] decided this was such a good idea he declared it a sin to be miserable or sick. So here we are. Slaves of a different form with no chance of escape."

"But cant' you protest?"

"The majority agreed it was the best thing for them as they feel secure behind these walls. They drink their faroc, made from fermented Catoa [that is the desert cactus common in these parts], and ......well I hope you now understand."

"But can you not all rebel and try to escape?"

"Long past it was when some of the Tarzonians returned to their mountains, but now if any of us tries, we are banished forever to the desert. The majority agrees that life is so good here it is no longer worth the risk. You will see there are no criminals and no one starves."

"But…"

"We have all we require," he added sardonically.

"But I could not bear it to laugh and smile against my will. That is preposterous."

"It is seen as a crime against the common good, and few see it otherwise now. If we appear perturbed the leaders feel we are a threat and we are watched closely. That is why Larrida was first so alarmed to see you."

"Then I have made a terrible mistake in entering your city, haven't I!"

Pretzel looked up in desperation but none of her flags were to be seen.

"You are here forever now. In time you will learn to like it here and then you will be less inclined to leave us."

"But all I did was to arrive and ask for a meal. Can't they see I am not one of them?"

"You will see some taller people who are offspring of travelers who came from the north. They could not escape either and in time accepted they were Saradens. You will feel the same one day."

Pretzel had to stop herself from retching.

"And what if a Saraden becomes ill? Do they still have to be cheerful?"

"They are put in the sick houses. It is seen an insult to the city if you are at all sick. Those people are called the Gracasses. Some never come back."

"I come from Grataco. I am a Gratacian. It sounds almost the same word."

"Then don't say you are a Gratacian or they might hear otherwise. Many are deaf from he hammering in the mines and it sounds too much the same."

"I'm glad you warned me. But what if you are dying?'"

"As I explained, they never come back."

"But what happens if your parents are about to die?"

"They know to smile a farewell then they join the Gracasses," added Larrida.

She blurted out these words quickly as if they didn't belong to her. Pretzel noticed her hands trembling.

"We must be seen to be doing good works. Never dare to look tired, worn, dispirited, lazy or angry."

The three stood on the balcony looking out at the forbidding walls.

"From where I come from, we are given a possum dog if we are sick, fed with healing breads and tarfaberry drinks until we recover. We are not punished for it!"

"Please don't raise your voice, Pretzel. Someone might hear you."

Pretzel heard a baby wailing below, and leant over to see the mother clap her hands over its mouth and rush back inside with him. She turned to face her hosts.

"That is monstrous!"

An icy chill ran down Pretzel's spine as she imagined the families separated by these heinous rules.

"The others are not like us," explained Tarod. "They approve of the system for as I said the city is kept peaceful, free of criminals and no good types."

"And where is the sick house?"

"See that path leading toward the south western corner. It slopes down and then there are steps going down to...that place. None can visit for it would darken their spirits. Aunt Brindel died there last year."

"And if I was to visit there?"

"You would not be coming back and if you were to try.... don't mention our names."

Pretzel looked into his face and saw tears in his eyes, which he wiped quickly away.

"Now we can't keep this conversation up for someone will get wind of it and we will all be in trouble. Let 's make our descent to the Square and you can see for yourself how well we live."

Pretzel was perplexed. At one moment her new friends seemed happy with their existence here and at another there was deep unrest. She chose not to ask any more questions for the moment for she felt she had challenged them enough.

An aroma of beef filled the air as they tramped down the narrow steps to the Square, but despite the delicious food, Pretzel could not enjoy the taste. The guffaws from the other tables now sounded forced. .

"You will become used to it," reassured Larrida.

It was not until they were home and safely out of range that Pretzel had to venture another question.

"You seem different from the others. Are you not?"

Tarod gave a long sigh and looked at Larrida who indicated him to continue.

"Yes, we are. Such is our fear of being noticed for it. I will explain as best I can. One day when we were out on farming duty we met some birds. We were surprised they began to speak to Larrida and me. What was more surprising however was that the other workers did not hear their words and when they saw our startled response to the birds they looked at us strangely. We knew then we would have to be careful. For loss of one's mind means joining the Gracasses."

Pretzel nodded her head. She felt an instant kinship with him as she was fearful of a similar thing happening to her in Grataco. She knew she would be treated with kindness, but no one would take her seriously ever again.

"How did you manage to talk to them if you were watched?"

"We could not, but we listened. The birds spoke of other lands. They taught us how to accept our feelings and to have another way of... being in the world. They told us that crying can be good and beautiful."

"Did they have names?"

"The one that taught us the most was Tach....."

"Tachymus?"

"Yes. You guessed right."

"What happened to them?"

"They were eventually chased away as they were seen as a threat for something about the way the birds looked at them made the Saradens uneasy. But we have we kept what they taught us to ourselves and live a different way of life in the safety of our home."

"I have met the very same birds but they are now far away for they needed the pine trees for safety."

"Oh." Larrida cried, grasping Pretzel's hand. "Then we can reminisce together, for I know they will no longer return to this place."

The three stood on the balcony looking down at the musicians playing cheerful sounding melodies on their high pitched reedy pipes. The Saradens joined hands, twirling faster and faster until they collapsed in delirious laughter.

Larrida sighed. "You will find it easier if you become one of us."

Pretzel looked at her in amazement.

"But you are not one of them."

"We try to be as best we can. For there is no way out of here... unless you are dead."

Pretzel gasped.

"No more questions now. We must sleep, for tomorrow you will come with me to see the fine rugs we are weaving. The women there are generous. They will teach you the Saraden knot which makes our rugs special. You will see how well we can enjoy each other's company."

It was though a switch had been turned off. Pretzel was given a square of matting on the balcony. She was glad to be out in the fresh air and needed to be alone in order to summon her flags, but there was no sign of them. It was not the first time that she wondered if she had dreamt them up in the first place and that they never really existed. There was nothing she could do, for to try to escape would place her hosts in danger. There was no choice but to become a 'Saraden' and bide her time. In the ensuing days she scanned the desert in the vain hope to see a wingflit or a passer by that she might manage to signal, but there was nothing bar the black eagles that daily soared above the city like an omen of death.

But after some weeks she became lulled into the daily routine. She felt nurtured by Larrida's warmth, reminding her more and more of Marthamum. She learned to play a strange ball game with the boys and their friends, being popular due to her height, to knot the fine goat wool, and to mix the wondrous hues more varied than Reza's silks. She became expert at dyeing the wool, crushing up the Catoa fruit to make subtle pinks and the stems to a brilliant lime green. She experimented with all manner of blends to the admiration of the women.

"She is becoming a true Saraden," Larrida exclaimed when Tarod arrived home to the evening meal.

He nodded his head wisely but said nothing, while the boys fiddled with their spoons and stared at their mother with vacant eyes.

But one night arrived when the full moon shone onto Pretzel's face. She stirred and sat up suddenly.

"Grataco!"

Larrida woke and came out to the balcony.

"You called out?"

"Yes, Grataco. This place is too like my village. We do not need walls to keep us in. But life is so good that no one wants to leave either. Is that so different?"

Tears rolled down her cheeks.

"Hush, Pretzi."

Pretzel felt as if Marthamum was soothing her, making her sobs uncontrollable.

"My dear, the time has come for you to leave us. It is dangerous for us all for you see too much."

As soon as dawn broke Larrida bundled up bread and fruit in a cloth and handed it to Pretzel.

"Follow the path to the Gracasses. You might find a way out."

"But only if I am dead." Pretzel whispered urgently.

Larrida led her to the door.

"You must go now."

"Say farewell and thanks to Tarod and....."

"We will tell them you have taken ill."

"Will I see you again?"

"Shhh. Go."

They held each other for a few seconds before Pretzel broke loose not looking behind her as she crept down the staircase into the grey morning.

CHAPTER 7   THE GRACASSES

A cold mist surrounded Pretzel as she tiptoed down the staircase into the streets, at present empty of Saradens. She looked up at the towers which loomed out of an eerie haze. A sudden boom of thunder echoed around her and as the first drops of rain fell she remembered Tarod describing the autumn storms and how the first rains are yellowed by the desert dust blown high in the wind. She started to run, her sac, bulging with Larrida's bread thumping on her back. She stopped to draw breath when the sun broke through. The towers shone like gold. Despite her wish to escape from them she was overcome by their beauty.

When she reached the outer city the towers were lower and less ornate. Suddenly she heard a clatter from a milk cart. She quickly put on the yellow shawl that Larrida had given her and knotted it in front in the Saraden way. She squatted down in the pretext of removing a stone from her shoe in order to disguise her height. The driver saw her and waved.

"Want a ride my girl?"

"No. I like the rain," Pretzel replied quickly and sighed with relief to see him climbing the stairs with his pail.

As soon as he was out of sight she hurried on through winding streets, but aiming southwards in the hope of soon reaching the far gate. She passed a group of miners waiting to leave for the morning shift, but they were too busy heaving their picks onto a truck for them to notice her. The towers lessened even more in height the more south she went, resembling large toadstools. Further on, she passed free standing homes made of pine logs. A cluster of women with brown woolen shawls stood round a stone tub where a communal fire was lit. They rubbed there hands and stamped their feet frequently to get warm. As soon as they saw Pretzel they all gave a quick smile of greeting yet she could sense their unease.

"They also think I'm a spy," she muttered and hurried on glad that they were too afraid to ask questions as to where she was going.

When she found what appeared like the Southern Gate it was firmly closed as she had dreaded it to be. Some how she had still hoped someone would open it for her like what seemed a lifetime ago. There was no sign of anyone, let alone a guard. She felt the impulse to hammer on the gate as she had done the first time, but thought it would be foolhardy to draw attention. Her only choice was to take the path to the hospital as Larrida had advised.

She could see it winding its way towards the south west corner, just as Larrida had described it. She reluctantly walked along it until she reached a clump of fig trees, their leaves glistening from the rain. Clusters of figs were beyond her reach. Pretzel thought it prudent to try climbing up to gather as much as she could carry for who knows whether she would find any food after the bread ran out. The climb was easy and she ate her fill before gathering the less ripe figs before clambering down. The last branch was covered in moss and her foot slid resulting in an awkward landing, twisting her ankle. She cursed and gathered up the broken off pieces of moss to wrap around it, recalling Marthamum's cold pack made up of splinters of ice wrapped up in a pillow slip. Pretzel limped painfully on with the added weight in her sac.

Two men pulling a trolley caught up to her. She could smell faroc on their breath, and noticed that their shirt and trousers were blood stained.

"Look here pretty girl! You can't walk too well can you!"

"It's just my ankle. I twisted it a bit…but it will recover very soon."

"You had better come with us."

She noted the filthy mattress on the trolley.

"I just need to rest until the swelling goes down."

"You are no use to any one the way you are."

"I can walk, truly."

The men laughed as Pretzel tried to walk normally, wincing with each step. The younger man eyed Pretzel appraisingly.

"A northern beauty, this one!"

"Looks won't help her here. Not if she can't work," the other added.

They lifted her on to the trolley, commenting on the length of her legs.

"She is a tall one."

The younger man chuckled at her discomfort.

"She talks funny too. They might hold you for ever, sweetie. They could do with young blood to cheer up those wretches."

"Come on. Stop ogling the girl. We have to collect a dead one."

They wheeled Pretzel on, bumping along the path until they reached an archway which led into a corridor before leaving Pretzel alone on her trolley with orders not to move. Her eyes slowly adjusted to the semi darkness. She wanted to get up and walk out but there was little point for there was nowhere she could hide. There were moans coming from behind the door and a stench of something rotten. When the two men reappeared they took no notice of Pretzel as she pulled herself up to see what was on their trolley. There was a shape covered in a sheet bar a white and wrinkled face protruding. The mouth was sunken. Pretzel had never seen a dead Gratacian, let alone a Saraden, and she wanted to be sick when the men wheeled the body past her. They whistled a tune as they disappeared through the archway.

Pretzel continued to lie there, trying to keep her mind off the poor Saraden. After what seemed hours she decided to investigate and limped down the corridor.

"Stay where you are!"

A woman opened the door and put her head round.

"I am Nurse Barrabesh. What is your illness?"

"I am not at all unwell. I have a twisted ankle, that's all."

The nurse walked out to examine Pretzel. She was wearing the traditional shawl, except it was a dirty grey draped over a long cardigan that was plain with none of the traditional stone inlay worn by the other Saradens she had met. Her clogs were enormous and the edges lined with goats wool. Pretzel guessed that this place would be freezing at night.

"It's a bit swollen, that's all. But we need workers here so you can stay. That will teach you for squealing.'

Pretzel bit her tongue.

"I am the chief nurse here and the only time I open my mouth is to give an order, so no nonsense. Do you hear me right?"

Pretzel tried to smile in the forced way that she had mastered, knowing it was safer not to complain.

Barrabesh dipped a thick needle into a purple solution and scraped a symbol on Pretzel's arm.

"Now you are a Gracass. You will remain here for as long as I think is necessary. My, you are a height. There are no beds to fit."

"I do not need a bed."

"What do you think you want? Special treatment?"

Pretzel made one more attempt.

"I hoped you might understand because you are a nurse, that I am not sick and do not need to stay in your hospital."

Barrabesh's large body shook with laughter.

"How many of these sickly souls have said that! You are no different from the others."

Pretzel squeezed her eyes to prevent her tears from escaping as Barrabesh scrutinized her.

"We have none of that blubbering here, girl. You surely know the rules. No Saraden worth their salt ever does that. They will be punished but I'll let you off this once."

She gave a chuckle at Pretzel's discomfort before leading her into a large circular room. Within it were beds placed like spokes on a wheel. In the centre was a huge desk with files neatly stacked. The headings were in a script that Pretzel had never seen before. There was that same rotten smell coming from a pile of bandages on the floor. The nurse pointed to the jug of water and a stone basin which lay under each bed.

"As soon as you can walk properly your job will be to fill these."

She pointed to the Saradens lying on their beds.

"Here are the rest of the Gracasses."

Some tried to sit up to take a better look at Pretzel as Nurse Barrabesh smiled.

"All of you must get fit or you are here for good. I like to see my Saraden patients get well so they can work again. Isn't that right, Gracasses?"

"Yes. Nurse Barrabesh," they replied in unison.

"This is where you sleep."

The sheets were covered in brown stains, and the bed much too short for Pretzel's length but she climbed onto it obediently, feeling more trapped than she had ever felt in her life.

"I will now put a compress on your ankle. It will heal quickly and then you will remain as long as I need an extra pair of hands. What a waste of time you are, limping about like this."

Barrabesh bound up Pretzel's foot with frayed length of bandage before bustling out of the room.

Pretzel surveyed her fellow Gracasses. Most of them were elderly but for a young man and woman who signaled to each other as soon as the nurse left the ward. She noticed that the door was ajar and through it shone a green light. The nurse's footsteps could be heard together with a clatter of bowls and hiccoughs. When the door eventually banged shut the girl went over to sit with the young man who coughed then spat into a mug. He was wasted, and his face had a grey pallor. Pretzel guessed that this illness was ebbing away at his strength.

"My name is Marokan," he spluttered, "I cannot stop this coughing so they will not let me out."

"Don't they have a cure for you?"

"She tried all her potions. None worked. I have to keep apart from my family now."

"From where I come from, they collect Tatuka leaves from around the lake. When my Poppo was ill, my mother boiled them up and he inhaled the fumes."

"So you are not a Saraden."

"No. I come from a village called Grat…I am not supposed to say its name…from a village across the desert."

The nurses' footsteps were heard returning so the girl retreated hurriedly to her bed. As soon as the nurse was out of earshot she rejoined Marokan.

"This is Bedua, my friend. She hurt her back falling off down the steps. She only speaks the old language which I guess you would not know. She returns home tomorrow as she has recovered sufficiently to work in the wash houses."

She had long black hair and her skin was pale compared to the bronzed weather-beaten look of her fellow Saradens.

"She comes from a family that does not venture outside much and do not mix with the others. They live on the edge of the city and are watched closely as they are considered a threat to us all. But I love her all the same."

Bedua gave a forced smile as she stroked Marokan's arm.

"I will not be seeing her again."

An old woman with eyes as opaque as the stones of Pradi sat on the edge of the bed feeling for her slippers. Pretzel handed them to her. The old woman said nothing, but reached for Pretzel's hand drawing it to her lips.

"Here comes our meal," announced Marokan.

A smell of onions filled the room, as Nurse Barrabesh appeared carrying a skillet filled with an oily looking broth swimming in some vegetable portions. The Gracasses that could walk crowded around, helping themselves in turn as Nurse watched. Bedua took a bowl over to the old lady as Pretzel sipped hers, making the most of the one piece of carrot in her bowl. As soon as Nurse Barrabesh left, Pretzel handed round Larrida's bread.

"Don't leave any crumbs or 'old bright eyes' will see," an old man called, stuffing the bread into his mouth.

"You must be an angel." Marokan added, smiling. However, Pretzel saw he only pecked at his, handing the remainder to Bedua.

In the afternoon light, the starkness of the grey walls and the chips in the wash basins were more evident. There was little for Pretzel to do but lie on her hard bed using her sac as a pillow and watch her companions. She was beginning to like this sad young man who had befriended her, and wondered about his illness.

The night seemed endless as Pretzel tossed and turned, longing to be home in her own bed, wishing this was just a nightmare. She had heard hiccoughing in the adjoining room throughout the night which suddenly ceased. This was followed by the shuffle of Nurse's shoes, men's voices and the rumble of a trolley. She felt sick at the thought of what it signified, and eventually fell into a restless sleep.

Next morning she woke to the smell of scrambled eggs.

"You will see plenty of this," muttered Marokan, "It's all we ever have for breakfast."

Pretzel pushed round the pale yellow material with her fork before forcing the rubbery texture into her mouth.

After several days, Nurse pushed on Pretzel's foot giving a wide grin.

"You are no longer a Gracass as you are fit enough to work. From now on you will sleep on a bunk in the kitchen. First you can collect the empty bowls and fill the jugs before preparing the vegetables. There are many onions to slice. That's a good job for cry babies."

Barrabesh laughed uproariously at her own joke as Pretzel felt it wiser to force a grin.

Pretzel went from bed to bed, mouthing a farewell to Marokan.

"I will visit when I can," she whispered as she collected his bowl, again barely touched.

The kitchen was spacious with a large chipped wooden table in the centre. A bunk, no doubt her sleeping quarters, was against one wall. Barrabesh gave instructions on how to light the stove. Pretzel gazed at the open shelves of pots, together with the meagre crockery and wondered at this city which had at first seemed so opulent. At first, she did not notice the bird cage hanging on the far wall until she heard a flutter. Pretzel ceased her chopping with surprise and went over to investigate and found a small bird with its tail feathers missing, and obviously thirsty. She brought over fresh water and sprinkled into the cage whatever remaining crumbs she had in her pocket. It came more to life and flapped its wings revealing the familiar green of the wingflits.

"Wow little bird. Can you also talk?"

The bird nodded and turned away quivering.

Nurse Barrabesh called out, "Who are you talking to?"

"I am counting out the vegetables," Pretzel replied, thinking quickly.

As soon as Barrabesh was out of range, Pretzel went over to the bird and whispered, "You are safe with me. I am not a Saraden. Can you talk now?"

"Dare not dare not."

"What are you doing here?" Pretzel whispered.

"They caught me. They caught all of us who were after the tomato seed. Tachymus, one of the birds......"

"But I know Tachymus and Batwin and….."

"Blow me feathers! Well as I was saying, Tachymus spoke to one family and taught them things…."

"You mean the family of Tarod?"

"Blow me feathers! My name is Freya. The Saradens chased us away but caught me and kept me here. They won't let me go."

"Why not?"

"They first put me in the ward so I might cheer up the Gracasses, speed their recovery so they can return to work."

"Why are you caged here then?"

"Nurse is trying to get me to talk She threatens to starve me if I won't. She goes over and over 'Pretty Saraden, Pretty Saraden,' till I am driven insane."

"I will try to get you out of here."

"Only one way out, if you are dead dead dead."

Barrabesh called out, "When you've finished, you can wash these bandages."

Pretzel returned to her kitchen duties feeling lighter of heart, but the days merged into weeks as Pretzel collapsed onto her bed with exhaustion each night. She guessed as the nights were becoming colder, Drako would be curling up with his possum dog for warmth. The flags were still silent and Pretzel frequently berated herself for abandoning them at that gate what seemed now an eternity. Pretzel believed she would die if it was not for her little friend Freya who gave her courage.

Marokan now was refusing all food and Barrabesh moved him into the room off the ward from which shone that greenish glow. One afternoon Marokan beckoned her in.

"Tonight I am dying. This is your only chance."

"What do you mean?"

"Nurse Barrabesh will pronounce me dead. Don't sleep. The men will come to collect me. They will transfer me from this bed onto the trolley. You must invite them into the kitchen, sit them down, laugh and joke with them, and offer them something to eat. When they are comfortable, return here quickly and put me under the bed, then climb on to the trolley and cover yourself with the sheet."

"But I can't leave you like that!"

"There is nothing more to say." Marokan took her hand." You must."

Pretzel stood looking into his sunken eyes, until Nurse called her. She carted in chunks of pine, placing it in the box by the fire, raced through her kitchen duties before whispering her plan to Freya.

"Eat as many crumbs as you can, for we are traveling far."

Pretzel filled her sac with what vegetables she could without them being missed before racing back to Marokan's side. She held his hand as it became colder. He was too weak to speak, but managed to open his eyes to give her a slow wink. Despite the rasping of his breathing, his face was peaceful.

That night, just as Marokan had predicted, his life ebbed away. Pretzel alerted Barrabesh who arranged for the assistants to remove his body. She ordered her to remain up until the men arrived with the trolley at first light. When at last they appeared, she watched, fighting back her tears, as they lifted his body with ease, commenting cheerfully how light it was, 'not like the last one.'

Pretzel swallowed her anger.

"Before you men leave, I have made a chicken soup for you."

They followed her into the kitchen where she seated them so that they faced away from the bird cage. After she had ladled out their soup and they were slurping hungrily, she secreted Freya in her pocket before returning to place Marokan's body under the bed. She pictured wherever he might be, giving one almighty chuckle as she stretched out on the trolley and placed the sheet over her being careful not to crush Freya. She dreaded that Barrabesh could wake up at any time and tensed with every scrape of the kitchen chairs.

At last the two men returned to take the trolley. She sensed each corner of the room that the trolley bumped into, heard the snores from the old lady by the window, felt the chill air hitting her like a stab wound as the trolley rumbled up the path, and saw the grey light of dawn through her lids. She heard the voices of the guards, and the key being turned in the lock and the wind as the gate was slowly heaved open.

The men chatted for what seemed an eternity as Pretzel lay still, barely breathing. They shared wine from their carafes which they drank with relish smacking their lips.

"What have you brought us tonight?" a guard enquired eventually, as he lifted the sheet back off Pretzel's face. She sat up in shock as the four men stared at her in amazement. Pretzel instinctively pulled out her topaz. The redness flickered onto the men's faces as they snatched it from her, passing it from one to the other.

Pretzel jumped off the trolley and grabbed her belongings before racing out into the brightness of day.

CHAPTER 8   THE RIVER

Pretzel hurried past the poplars that bordered the city's walls
and on until she came to a nest of brambles in which to hide.
All was silent. She guessed the guards were squabbling over
the topaz which was more important than recapturing the tall
woman that had materialized out of the trolley. When she
felt it safe she scrambled out, tearing her skin badly but she
barely noticed as she sprinted over open grasslands where
a herd of cattle looked up with surprise. She reached a forest of trees and glanced behind but still no guards in sight,
so stopped to catch her breath. The towers loomed behind
her. They had no magic for her any more, seeing their stark
whiteness holding such oppression within their walls. She
breathed in fresh air in long slow gulps, delighting in the
warm sun on her face.

She felt Freya's trembling through her pocket and at last
was able to lift her out and place her on the ground. The bird
closed her eyes with the shock of seeing brightness of day for
the first time for so long, and as soon as she came accustomed to
the light, flapped her wings uncertainly.

Pretzel suddenly sensed a swaying sensation around her
and looked around her with amazement to see that her flags had
returned.

"You waited for me."

"What do you expect?"

"I should have listened to you."

"It appears not."

Pretzel looked at Freya who was already beginning to hop and peck at insects.

"I would never have rescued her if I had listened to you."

"Those that always obey our good sense miss out."

"How then do I know when to listen to you?"

"You listen and then you decide what you will do."

"It is really up to me then, flags. You mean I can't rely on you after all."

The flags waved her away as if they were tired of any more of this conversation. Pretzel shrugged, happy that this was the longest dialogue she had ever had with these somewhat uncommunicative guides.

She munched on a carrot and held out bird seed for Freya who soon became agitated.

"We must get away from this horrible city, Pretzel. I am flying. Watch me."

It was a delight to see that already her little friend who had been silenced for so long was regaining her confidence as she dipped and dived around her.

"Please stop, Freya. You're making me dizzy."

Freya chirped louder, her patience running out, so Pretzel dragged herself up. They followed a winding track that disappeared under trailing plants. Freya flew ahead to show the way but tired easily and needed to rest frequently until she discovered a small pool of water in a rock. She immersed herself with glee and out emerged a much brighter bird, the green under her wings glinting, her beak now a bright yellow and the blackness of her feathers rich and deep.

"You are really a wingflit ...well, almost..."

Freya's tail feathers would take some weeks to grow.

By afternoon they arrived at a grove of tall pines. Pretzel picked out a dry patch to camp and searched through her food supply which comprised mainly of onions which made her eyes water. She had to reassure Freya she was not sad, and as for her breath, Freya avoided being anywhere nearby until the 'meal 'was complete. Despite a few remaining limp carrots, there was still plenty of birdseed for Freya. She offered to share them with Pretzel.

"Thanks, but I am not a bird,"

Pretzel wished at this moment she was one, for how much easier it would be to find food in the forest. She fantasized a large serve of roast chicken and immediately felt guilty. It would be most improper to mention it in the company of a wingflit.

But as she explored the valley, Pretzel noticed a patch of moss sprouting the same pink flowers that was the delicacy that Saradens used in their salads. She sucked on the stems, relishing the citrus flavour, startling Freya as she grinned at her with crimson stained teeth.

The sun was sinking fast. Pretzel crawled into her cocoon sac relishing the sound of the wind through the trees. Freya waited until Pretzel's eyes were closed before flying onto an overhanging branch to sleep, nestling her beak into her wing which now had the aroma of bird instead of being contaminated by that putrid hospital smell. She woke at times to hear Pretzels' comfortable breathing, impressed how this tall human being was able to find any makeshift bed for comfort, this one being a mattress of plants and stones. Freya had always felt sorry for animals that could not sleep standing up and how hard it would be to find a place to sleep when traveling long distances. Birds could easily find a tree or small cave somewhere. She mused on this as her bird thoughts circled round in her head which was disappearing more and more into her downy feathers. She did not hear the fluttering of wings in the trees around her, but slept until the dawn had changed from pink to yellow.

As for Pretzel, she stirred a few times to pull out another flower to suck through her lips, before falling into the warm black pit of sleep. When the light became grey through her lids she woke to see a yellow beak peering at her.

"Why, Freya! You are awake and ready to go?"

"What what what." called Freya from the branch, her sleepy eyes still nestled in her wing.

Pretzel sat up with a start.

"Tachymus!"

He peered at her closely while the rest of the wingflits twittered excitedly at the discovery of their old friend.

Freya woke complaining about the morning noise, but when she looked down she saw the entire company of wingflits greeting Pretzel who was weeping with joy as each bird in turn fluttered their 'hello' on her cheek. Sorro somersaulted with joy, Batwin shook his head from side to side in disbelief, while Roland who had been high in the sky scouting for danger, fluttered down to see what the fuss was about. Freya called to them from her branch in a high trill. If birds could cry, they would have surely. Pretzel was now forgotten as they crushed in around Freya, who had practically fallen off her branch in such haste to land on the ground amongst them. She fluffed up her feathers with emotion as one by one the wingflits one at a time allowed her to place her small head on their wing.

Batwin shook his head at Freya, "We thought you must have been dead by now."

The wingflits listened with awe as Freya described her dreadful incarceration in the hospital; how the nurse had caged her and tried to make her talk, how she had so many times nearly died of either starvation or boredom and how the arrival of Pretzel had given her the will to live again. Batwin was particularly impressed how the very same stone that he had used to save

Pretzel from drowning in the desert sand had enabled them both to escape from Saraden City. The wingflits wanted to hear more of Freya's adventures but by now the sun was high in the sky and Tachymus announced it was time to continue on through the forest where there was plenty of nesting places.

"We will not let you leave us again." Batwin commanded sternly. "No more deserts, and what's more avoid cities at all cost!"

Pretzel was deeply touched by her earnest little friend. Tachymus flew around her, commenting on how thin she was. He offered her a worm which she politely declined. It was not always easy explaining that her food requirements differed from theirs.

"Look over there, Tachymus. Those flowers will do for my meal!"

Tachymus commanded the wingflits to help Pretzel. They flew off in all directions, gathering the small flowers into their beaks and attaching others to their feet as Pretzel picked them off each bird, placing them in her sac. Not till her sac and pockets were full did he allow the group to continue on their way. They were about to make a start when a pink fluffy creature thumped into the centre of the group, barely able to stand.

"Oh, Sorro!"

He had rolled in a sticky bush, before collecting the flowers which had stuck to every part of his body. Pretzel removed them one by one while the rest chirped with admiration.

"Trust Sorro," she cried, stroking down his feathers, "How I have missed you."

The air was cold under the trees. Pretzel pulled on Reza's pyjamas which the wingflits found hilarious for she reminded them of a large Tarzon macaw. They flitted around her with glee as Pretzel walked on. In this manner the group trudged and flew, squawking and hooting for days until one afternoon Pretzel chose to halt at a grassy bank.

"I need time to listen to my flags for I have been forgetting them in all my excitement at being with you all again."

The wingflits surveyed her as she curled up in her sac, while Freya remained on a low branch singing a song barely audible to Pretzel who soon fell into a long sleep. She dreamt that she had reached the end of a long journey. She was standing looking into the blackest deepest chasm and woke with fright, but when she heard Freya's soft chirps that reassured her it was safe to sleep again. The flags remained in the background until Pretzel was fully awake.

"This path will take you to...where you must go."

"And where is that?"

Pretzel could get no further answers from them and decided she would no longer worry. But for that brief moment of fear in her dream, she was the happiest she had ever been since leaving Grataco. She had surprised herself that she was not feeling at all homesick for her family, in fact had barely given much thought of her village since she had escaped from the Saradens. The woods gave out a gentle hush, only broken by the noisy fluttering of wingflits as they flapped and squawked over their favourite places. Pretzel gazed up at the trees where a lacework of stars peered through. As soon as it was morning she was keen to get started for her pyjamas were sodden with dew.

"I wish I had built in dry clothes like you lot," she laughed, rubbing pieces of grass off her clothes.

It amazed her how fast they were back to being a family again as if nothing had happened since that sad farewell at the desert's edge.

Freya admired Batwin's domed beak.

"From carving away the topaz from deep tunnels."

She was enthralled by his story how he had worked alone in the dark of those underground mines. There was so much she had missed during her time in Saraden City and she looked forward to being kept entertained by their stories for a lifetime.

"And what of the Hetzenbabel? Is it still alive?"

She blocked out with her feathers the description of the manner it had grown to kill and devour her friends and relatives.

When it was time to move on, Sorro as usual spent the longest time pirouetting about before preening his feathers. Roland scouted the land ahead and Tachymus checked out and approved of Pretzel's sac, which was now plump with flowers. Pretzel made her way beneath the pines as the wingflits flew above except for Freya who hopped along with Pretzel to keep her company. Late afternoon Roland landed amongst them, feathers damp and flapping excitedly.

"One big river!" was all he could squawk until he had collected his breath.

Pretzel hurried her pace until she could see glimpses of water through the trees. She imagined it might be like Lake Grataco but when she reached it, the banks were slippery with black mud, and the water was a deep green and flowing rapidly with numerous whirlpools out in the middle. She slithered down the bank to feel the water which was cold as ice, and threw in a stick which immediately was whisked away downstream.

"So this is the river Banzoor that my flags have sung of. Can you see where I can cross, Roland?"

He spoke in a tone as if talking to one of their fledglings, "You swim. We fly."

"See how the current is flowing. It is far too strong."

"There is a path on the other side. You are meant to cross it. That's all."

"You must understand, Roland. I don't have wings like you, and I have only learned to frog kick."

With that the wingflits shared frog jokes that Pretzel did not see was at all funny under the circumstances.

"Swim it, swim it." chirped Sorro, bobbing his head out of the water as he experimented with all manner of landings before shaking water over Pretzel

She wiped the drops off herself crossly, "I will drown. It is too wide, too strong, and too cold. It can't be done."

Roland, bird of few words, stood and stared at her, shaking his head from side to side in exasperation.

"Alright then, if you don't care if I drown then, just watch me!"

Pretzel slithered down the bank and stood on the edge before wading in until the water was up to her thighs. She felt its tug on her as she took another step in and instantly lost her footing before being swept down stream. The wingflits followed her, squawking loudly as she struggled to reach the bank, many times missing her footing again in the slippery mud. She eventually scrambled up covered in mud and gasping for breath.

"I felt the pull of the deep. Can you not understand I am not ready to die yet?"

Freya flew to her shoulder as she peeled off her pyjamas and wrapped herself in her cocoon sac.

"Tachymus! You have to think of something." Freya twittered, refusing to leave Pretzel's side.

"It is time to rest. I will think tomorrow," he said gravely.

The wingflits quietly helped Pretzel gather dry twigs for her to sleep on to prevent her sliding into the water in the middle of the night. Freya helped arrange them as the rest nested above.

"No desert sands, no Saradens, no Gracasses, no Gatekeepers, just a river, and it has me beaten, Freya."

The river looked eerier when lit by a half moon: a treacherous black ribbon sweeping past her. Pretzel had heard tales of how rivers were far less trustworthy than oceans, for if you ventured out, the waves would bring you back, but rivers take you away for ever. She had only ever seen the small mountain streams that could be jumped across. And as for Lake Grataco, it was placid and reliable. But here she was trapped again.

As soon as it was morning Pretzel felt instantly cheered by Sorro who dipped his beak into the water, making gurgling sounds of delight., but then Roland returned reporting he had seen a group of very large animals upstream and it would not be wise for a creature that was not able to fly to go that way.

"You could build a boat." he suggested.

Pretzel thumped her hand on a trunk.

"I don't have the tools to chop a tree down."

Batwin displayed his beak.

"Yes I know you would do it eventually Batwin but it would take years and years for your beak to saw through one of these."

Batwin looked put out.

"No hard feelings please, Batwin. I am just trying to say.......I will continue up river despite those beasts. Who knows! They may be friendly anyway."

The flags began to wave frantically above her.

"Stay where you are."

She remained on the bank feeling that this time she was meant to listen to them, but when the sun was high in the sky and beat down on her, and when a large fly landed on and stung her face, she slapped at it, fighting back tears.

"Chahoots wacko wacko woy!"

She looked up with surprise at the sound coming from the middle of the river. A figure was perched on a raft and as it came closer, Pretzel could see it was an old woman steering a mattress effortlessly against the current using a broom as her paddle. Yellow hair stuck out from her head in similar fashion to the Festival clowns. Long thin legs protruded out of a tattered maroon dress displaying knees which were large and misshapen. She frequently dipped one end of her cloak into the river, squeezing it out to wipe her face. When almost at the bank, the old woman reached into the river and grabbed a fish which she gleefully swallowed in one gulp, spitting out the fins, before swirling the mattress to where Pretzel sat open mouthed.

"Get in. Get in. You can't stay here all day," she ordered in a harsh wine, looking dubiously at the wingflits circling round Pretzel.

"Migods! Who are you all? Can't say I'm partial to puny little birds like these. No good for a casserole."

Pretzel noted her flags waving approvingly so she ignored the old lady's suggestion that her friends could be food and rolled up her baggage before placing one foot gingerly in the centre of the mattress. She nearly lost her footing which caused a collection of water as the improbable craft dipped precariously from side to side.

"Now see what you've done! "

The old woman paddled to the centre of the river while Pretzel hung on for grim death. She deftly steered it round huge whirlpools just a hands breadth away. As they continued swirling towards the other side, the wingflits flew dutifully behind.

CHAPTER 9   HARRAGAR

By the time they reached the opposite bank, Pretzel was laughing and chortling along with Harragar as if they had been friends from long ago. However, when she stepped off into the mud which sucked at her ankles, memories flooded back until she noticed the old woman's large footprints continuing on up the slope.

"You won't sink in girl!" reassured Harragar, "How was the ride?"

"I've never I crossed a river like this before. Where I come from there are just small mountain..."

"I can't hear a thing you're saying for those birds. What's your name? You'll have to yell."

"Pretzel, short for Prêtzova."

"Each to their own! I'm Harragar."

"And this is Sorro and Batwin and....."

"You'll be calling the trees names next! Give me a hand, gal."

Pretzel helped drag the mattress up the bank. She slipped and slid in her shoes, noticing that Harragar's splayed feet with their long toenails were of advantage here to grip in the mud. Harragar pulled up her skirt around her and Pretzel could not help staring at her knees that looked as if they were padded with excess tissue. Otherwise the old woman was tall and thin with an upright posture.

"Some used to call me Harragar the Dread Witch."

"Why did they call you that?"

"Those who didn't know any better."

Harragar found a stump and sat busily scratching the mud off her feet with a stick while Pretzel looked on in silence, uncertain what to say next.

"So you're lost!"

"Not exactly, well sort of...."

"They turn back when they see me but you waited for me."

Pretzel felt it impolite to ask how she could possibly know she was waiting for her when she didn't know the old witch existed anyway but it was all too difficult and confusing for the woman was treating her like an expected guest.

"I know that you were waiting."

"How?"

Harragar looked far away as she hummed to herself.

"Well, we were camping in the forest and we came across this river ..."

"The River Banzoor."

"And we...I was going to turn around as there was no way across and.....that's all."

She was not ready to explain that the reason for her being here was because of her flags. She feared she would be mocked by this old lady who seemed friendly enough, but she found it unnerving that Harragar seemed to know more about her than she did herself.

Harragar threw a pine cone at Tachymus.

"Gid off!"

"No! Please! They're my friends."

"Well, they can keep their distance and stay up in the trees. That's what birds are for. I don't want them flapping round me. Anyway they're no good for a roast."

Pretzel looked horrified until she picked a twinkle in the old woman's eyes.

"But I have a turkey."

Pretzel fought a war inside herself. How could she eat a bird ever again but her stomach was rumbling. The wingflits had already settled in a grove of pine trees and to Pretzel's relief were out of hearing range. They came up to a vine laden with berries which some of the wingflits had already discovered as they hovered around the crimson fruit. Harragar picked up another pine cone ready to hurl it in their direction.

"There are many more vines and those are mine."

She laughed at Pretzel's alarmed face, thumping her on the back so hard that she nearly lost her footing.

"Don't worry, girl. The forest creatures know where they stand with me."

When Pretzel saw the rope ladder hanging from one of the branches, she could see why the old woman was so protective of these particular fruit. It looked a difficult climb even for a child. Harragar walked on until a coil of smoke appeared to be rising from a pile of rocks.

"Shoes outside!"

Pretzel was glad to pull off her shoes which had crusted inside and were beginning to rub. She followed Harragar into what appeared to be a cave but as her eyes became accustomed to the light, she could see that it was actually a dwelling built behind the rocks, cleverly concealed. Harragar pulled aside thick woollen curtains to reveal a large room with a kitchen table comprising a chunk of wood balancing on logs. Alongside it was a fire which glowed red from burning pine cones. The other end of the room was taken up with a huge and bulky mattress that took the shape of Harragar's knobbly frame. Outside the back door was a washing line strewn between the bushes and from which hung long yellowed under garments. Harragar began to strip off her dress and step under a waterfall which cascaded down through a gap in the rocks. She splashed her face before immersing herself while Pretzel tried not to stare at the old lady's breasts which were pendulous and reaching her navel. Harragar beckoned her to follow suit and at last Pretzel's hair felt light again. She handed her a blue dress for her to wear which reached to the ground reminding Pretzel of Marthamum's housecoats which she dressed up in as a child.

"Time to wash those 'pyjama' things, girl. They're a right sticky mess. You'll attract all the bees in the forest."

Batwin landed on the roof briefly before flying off. Pretzel felt comforted that the wingflits were checking up on her welfare.

Harragar ladled out thick potato soup followed by the promised turkey which Pretzel devoured with gusto. She then sliced up a pie filled with the stewed berries and watched with bemusement her guest demolishing these also as if she had never set eyes on food before. After their second helpings, Harragar poured a black drink into little stone ramekins. It tasted of liquorice and soon Pretzel felt languid and could not keep her eyes open despite efforts to make an attempt at polite conversation.

"Rest over there, gal."

Pretzel crawled to one end of the mattress and fell immediately asleep, her breaths becoming quiet and deep. Harragar leant over her and watched her, making sucking sounds through the gaps in her teeth as she dribbled on Pretzel who was past being concerned about the old lady's habits.

Pretzel remained curled up until the early hours of the morning when she woke for a brief moment to get her bearings. There was no sign of Harragar. For the first time she had left Grataco, she felt homesick, and lay there staring up at the pinie planks on the ceiling, envisaging Drako starting another term at school. She imagined her mother in a blue house coat, the same as she was now wearing, ladling out the soup with Poppo seated at the table looking grim and thoughtful. She then switched her thoughts to the swirling black river Banzoor and began to shake violently until she became aware that her flags were above her waving gently to and fro.

She slept again and did not wake until mid afternoon. The fire was crackling brightly as the golden sun's rays streamed through the back door. There was still no sign of Harragar. Pretzel stumbled out into the back garden to see that her scarf, socks and pyjamas had been washed and were drying on the line. In the distance was the sound of rushing water mingled with loud shrieks and whoops echoing round the trees.

Pretzel followed the sound and found a trail leading round the side of the house towards an embankment. From there she could see Harragar standing above a huge waterfall. She watched Harragar bending down before seating herself onto a mattress and gasped with horror as she pushed herself off and over the edge. Harragar shrieked with glee as she bounced onto the rocks before landing below in a deep pool, lying there to catch her breath before clambering up the side of the waterfall. She then repeated the same exercise over and over, always accompanied by loud hoots. Eventually Harragar looked up from the pool and saw Pretzel.

"Come girl! Grab a mattress! "

On the bank lay another of these ubiquitous objects. Pretzel dragged the heavy mattress to the top of the waterfall. She stared at the pool so far below and despite Harragar's encouragement kept balking until Sorro suddenly appeared. He flew around her and was soon followed by the rest of the wingflits.

"Take off!" chirped Sorro as Pretzel felt she was a fledgling taking her first flight.

She closed her eyes and pushed off, feeling as if she was leaping to her death, but bounced with ease over the rocks before arriving with a splash alongside Harragar. Pretzel now understood why Harragar had such huge padded knees which were ideal for this kind of sport. Now that Pretzel was confident she would remain in one piece the two of them repeated the climb and slid together down the waterfall over and over until Harragar stood up.

"Time for another feed, gal. You are thin and out of condition."

She hurried home, leaving Pretzel to empty the mattresses of water before dragging them up the slope. By the time she had arrived back to the hut, Harragar had already prepared more vegetables before boiling up the turkey remains. Pretzel could hear the familiar twittering of the wingflits outside and hoped they would not come any closer until the bones had been well picked. As they both sat spooning their meal from bowls, Pretzel questioned Harragar.

"How is it that you are living here alone in the forest?"

"It is my home, gal. I found this place or …it found me. More of that later… Can I call you Pretzi? You look Pretzi-ish."

Pretzel had almost forgotten what she looked like, let alone what a Pretzi was supposed to resemble. She guessed the skin on her face was as brown as her arms and after her wash, she could see the fronds of her hair were a shiny black again.

"Let me plait it for you." Harragar asked.

"I…have come of age. It must be worn out….but I no longer care. Yes. Please plait it Harragar. I would like that."

Nightfall came quickly. Harragar shook out her mattress and indicated a place for Pretzel before falling asleep. Pretzel eked out as much of the corner of the bed as she could whilst avoiding Harragar's dribble. She listened to the old woman's breathing and wondered more and more what mysterious circumstance had brought her here, for it seemed she was not going to be forthcoming in an explanation. There were so many questions she wanted to ask. She lay awake listening as Harragar's snores became lighter, followed by a strange muttering before calling out, "You are on your way to find the Wattoo and will never be the same. Like me, you will never be the same." Some of them were in such a low voice as barely audible. She talked of a foreign place over and over throughout the night until at last she stirred, singing in a guttural voice,

"The mountain is high
The mountain is bare.
The going is steep.
You will find the Wattoo."

She sung this over and over until her eyelids t flickered before returning into heavy sleep.

In the early hours of the morning Pretzel at last tried to sleep, but just as her eyes began to close, Harragar jumped up.

"Time to light the fire, gal. Bring me in some pine cones... Come on, Pretzi girl, you've slept enough."

"Well, no I didn't...because you were talking ..."

"So you were listening in, hey?"

"Not on purpose...but I couldn't help it.....do you mind if I ask....what is the Watt...."

"Shhh"

Harragar began to hum to herself.

"You'll find out when you're ready me gal."

Harragar stared into the fire. Her voice was barely audible.

"But you will never find it unless you follow."

Meanwhile the flags waved slowly above her as if in awe.

CHAPTER 10   THE GOAT THIEF

Next morning Pretzel was eager to hear Harragar's description of her journey up that mountain but it was as if the conversation had never existed. Harragar sang quietly to herself as she filled the pots with fresh water from the stream before throwing in the turkey bones for lunchtime soup. They both sat in silence eating a breakfast of thick bread wrapped around fresh pine nuts. Pretzel assumed there would be no butter or milk due to the absence of farm animals but she was mistaken. A faint bleating came from the top of the hill.

"Me goats! Oh me goats!"

Harragar pulled out a huge handkerchief and blew her nose before shaking her fist in the air.

"Let me warn you, my girl. Don't ever think of venturing over the hill. There are this group of men that live over there. Terrible folk they are. Just terrible! These men sneak up and steal my goats. This time all but one is left and is now too afraid to come down. Spooked it is!"

Pretzel saw for the first time a mixture of anger and fear in Harragar's eyes. It had seemed to her that this old woman was invincible, but as she had learned from meeting the Saradens, nothing is ever as it seems at first. How she wished that Poppo was here, for he would know what to do. Poppo always managed to find their goats if they were lost, even if he had to take days to coax them out of deep crevices in the rock.

"They live in the swamplands and despite all the mosquitoes, stay living close to the river where there is no need to cart water. They can't be bothered to grow crops. Instead they steal my goats when they wander over the hill to find new grass, milk the poor little things dry, and then let them go. Some might return to me, but they are no further use for milking for they are too afraid."

Harragar's eyes brimmed again as Pretzel passed her a tea towel to dry them.

"The new goats I find on the other side of The Banzoor and I coax them on to my mattress, but some wander off and I won't paddock them. Not these. They love their freedom too much. They need rocks to climb. They had plenty of good stream water but those men lure them somehow... or perhaps they like too much the bracken that grows around the swamp."

"Who are those people?"

"I know nothing about them as they refuse to have anything to do with me. I suspect they were trapped after the earthquake but they prefer to stay where they are rather than befriend an old lady. I heard them talking once and the dialect sounds to me they are from the east. See those razor back mountains. That is the eastern chain of the Goplin Thirkins and they have changed their shape since the last quake of about twenty years ago."

"Why would they not try to go home?"

"Perhaps there is nothing to go home to if it is all obliterated. All the women and children."

Pretzel shuddered with horror. "Those poor men,"

"I know it is dreadful and all but...and I felt sorry for them at first but ....Don't you go anywhere near that place. Not you. Not a young one like you, pretty and all."

The bleating sounded more desperate.

"Harragar! My bird friends.....They might be able to help you. Does your goat have a name?"

Harragar smiled through her tears.

"Well. I see all your feathered friends have names. Her name is Martha."

"That's my mother's name... Marthamum....If only she knew about you."

Pretzel wondered though how her mother would react if she was to met Harragar. On one hand Marthamum would appreciate her taking on the grandmother role, yet she was nothing like old Varsla who was always conscious of her manners. Harragar was like none she had ever met before. Was it her looks? Her dress? No, more than that. There appeared to be no rules that Harragar obeyed except her own.

"You are a long way from home, aren't you?"

"Yes, you can say that."

"Where are you traveling to, girl?"

"I do not know. It's just... I... needed to leave."

"What was the matter, gal?"

"Nothing, really. No one forced me to go. I upset them all as I needed to follow my fla ....find an adventure."

"Dreams eh?"

"Yes, you can say that."

"I had those too." Harragar murmured.

"What happened?"

Harragar's eyes had a far away look.

"You follow them. You find them out. You have to be brave, you have to be steadfast, you have to be stubborn...then you find out."

"There are these flags that lead me."

"Listen gal, listen. Careful who you tell."

"Why?"

"Thems what you tell will want to stop you, or they will think you are crazy and lock you away, or they will laugh at you, or want to harm you, or all manner of things."

"But I have told you now."

Harragar took Pretzel's arm.

"What you tell me is safe with me. I would never mock you or think you are off your tree."

She jumped up.

"Come on. Show me what your bird friends can do. We're going to get that goat before those men get mine."

Harragar and Pretzel scrambled up in the direction of the bleating.

"Wingflits! Batwin, Tachymus!"

Harragar stamped and chuckled. "Tachym.....sounds so learned heh!"

"He knows a lot."

The birds arrived in a spiral formation just as Pretzel had first seen them by the lake last spring. She now knew it was their way of appearing formal when in unknown situations or when meeting a stranger. They were still wary, but when Tachymus saw the way Pretzel talked with Harragar, he fluttered down.

"Tachymus, I would like to formally introduce you to Harragar."

He was followed by the rest of the wingflits, who flew one by one over Harragar's head as she tried to keep a straight face and nodding politely as she hung on to a branch of a tree.

"I'm becoming. dizzy! Don't take all day. We need to find this goat."

How Pretzel relished Harragar's lack of niceties. She felt for the first time in her life she would be able to pick her teeth, dance silly dances whenever she felt like, and screech out songs without a care.

The bleats were now coming from the undergrowth much to Harragar's dismay.

"May those mud men stick in their own mire and sink!"

"Tachymus will fly around your goat and turn it around."

"Watch out! Those good for nothings carry sharp axes."

Harragar was breathing heavily after their steep climb. She brushed at her shoulder until she realized that it was Freya perching there.

"We will get your goat." Freya trilled.

Harragar laughed despite her anxiety.

"Be quick, then."

The wingflits disappeared into the scrub while Pretzel and Harragar watched.

Soon there was louder bleating mingled with shouts. Harragar raced towards the path to meet the goat as it bounded out from the trees, the wingflits flapping behind. In their wake stumbled a foul smelling man who stopped in surprise as Batwin flew at him and pecked his ear. He stared at them through blood shot eyes, and wiped green mucus pouring from one nostril with the back of his hand before lurching at the wingflits but they were far too quick for him. He lost his balance, falling backwards onto a rock. His axe flew off to wedge into the branches. Harragar yanked it out and ran her fingers along the blade.

"Could do with a new one" she puffed.

"What about him?"

"His mates will drag him back. They won't dare to come out for a while. Cowards. But they'll be back and they'll be mad....very mad."

"Is he dead?"

"Wish he was. He'll just have a sore skull. They're built like tree trunks."

"The wingflits will keep watch. Roland is already up there scouting."

Pretzel pointed out his flying pattern which was in a circle before bobbing up and down, signaling that all was safe, but they weren't taking any chances. Martha spent the night inside, after being scrubbed clean, and fed with the choicest vegetables topped with peanuts, finishing off her meal with succulent red berries. Harragar lit no candles and they ate in silence.

They both kept waking to make a fuss of the goat. It was a handsome creature now it had been cleaned up, revealing long cream hair, a rounded nose and a short brown tail which quivered constantly. Pretzel felt the soft muzzle and that familiar warm breath on her face. By morning, the udder was full, and a sweet smell of goat's milk filled the room. Harragar slept, snoring noisily until the sun was well up, while Pretzel milked Martha, reliving her early morning duty in Grataco. Life felt so good, she wanted this moment to last for ever but eventually her eyelids drooped and she fell into a deeper sleep.

She dreamt of a still morning in Grataco where Marthamum sat milking. Suddenly the goat became restless, jumping this way and that. She then began to sing to it, lulling it to be still, stroking it firmly and rubbing her fingers between the animal's ears. She fondled its soft hair and began to comb its hair with long strokes.

Pretzel woke remembering her mother combing her own long hair many months ago. She reached out for Martha and buried her face in her soft fur.

CHAPTER 11   THE DELL

When Harragar woke, she rubbed her aching legs and reached for her brush. She scraped it through the tangles before gathering them into a bun which she looped around with twine.

"I can smell the milk, gal."

Pretzel carried over a mug filled to the brim with warm goats' milk, and Harragar murmured with pleasure between gulps, looking out at Martha who was now munching the grass in the back enclosure, her tail quivering with pleasure.

"Our family is complete at last."

"It is," Pretzel replied, watching Martha's antics and wishing that she could stay and be a part of it for ever, but the restlessness in the pit of her belly was disturbing. It had invaded the peace of this morning when her flags competed for her attention. Despite her growing fondness for Harragar, the way of life deep in the forest and the added thrill of sliding down waterfalls, she knew it would be increasingly difficult to leave if she was to settle in too well.

Harragar noticed Pretzel's melancholy.

"Put your boots on for I am going to show you a special place."

Pretzel appreciated the distraction from her thoughts as Harragar was already out the door and heading down the track. Pretzel hurried behind, her shoelaces trailing, and caught up with her.

"Aren't you afraid the goat thief will attack us?"

"We will cross the stream where it narrows and double back. We won't be anywhere near those trouble makers."

She leapt over the stream with agility. It seemed so simple with her long legs and toes. Pretzel chose to wade tentatively rather than risk slipping on the rocks.

"You're not used to this, gal."

"Not with water bubbling round me like this. It's too slippery."

Harragar threw a tomato to Pretzel which she missed and it squirted down her clothes in her effort to catch it and balance at the same time.

"You could have waited until I caught up!"

This time Pretzel was ready for her as she fielded the second tomato until they were both dripping with juice.

"Oh, the bees will love us. Follow me now."

She strode on ahead before disappearing amongst the trees.

"Over here!"

Pretzel parted the branches and followed in the direction of Harragar's voice until she found she was bathed in bright sunlight. Vines cascaded over logs and twined up trees, forming a curtain which separated them from the rest of the forest. On the ground were crimson daisies as large as her hand, while dotted amongst them peeped deep blue flowers in the shape of tiny snails. In the corner of the clearing, stood Harragar, licking the fluid which dripped from pale yellow berries and ignoring the bees hovering around her. Pretzel kicked off her boots, feeling the coolness of the grass between her toes before joining Harragar who proudly showed a patch of earth where she was cultivating potatoes and melons, one of which Harragar split open. The deep pink flesh was delicious.

"No one knows about this place, not even the goats."

They both lay down on the grass, the sun warming their faces.

"I could stay here forever."

"Them's the likes of you can't. Sad enough it is, girl."

Pretzel sighed inwardly with relief, for now she could broach the subject of her leaving.

"I know that restlessness. When I left the ocean and came to the mountains, only then I was…this is my home, now."

"So this is where you stay now, for ever?"

"This is not your place, gal. You must…"

"What must I do?"

"You must avoid those mudmen first. Follow the goat tracks round the western side of the hill away from the river. You will have to carry plenty of water for you will need to give it a wide berth till you are far upstream."

Pretzel was confused, for the flags had been pointing directly along its banks. The last time she ignored them and went in an opposite direction, she had become a captive in Saraden City.

She felt nonplussed until suddenly she had an idea.

"Harragar! You've been up the mountain to that place you talk of in your sleep, haven't you? The Wattoo."

"Shhh!"

"It's a wonder I haven't thought of it before. Why don't you come with me?"

"No, Pretzi. And that's that. In any case I am getting old now."

She began to hum, which indicated it was the end of any further discussion. Pretzel was beginning to read those hums like a book. Harragar heaved herself up and began filling her voluminous pockets with potatoes.

"You are not that old. You are stronger than me!"

"No, my girl. It's when the cold hits. In winter I'm a different kettle of fish. All coiling up and muttering and sitting stoking the fire all day and shivering and grumbling and rubbing my legs and toes with chilblains as big as rocks."

"Just some of the way, then?"

"Wheedling gets you nowhere. Have a potato."

Harragar held out one which Pretzel refused.

"I don't eat them raw!"

"You will have to learn to. There's no fire out there to boil them up."

She took Pretzel's arm, "Listen, Pretzi, you are scared I know."

"No, I'm not!"

"Yes, I thought you were a cool fish but now I know you better."

Harragar began her humming again.

"If you say you're scared, you can….then you can go on till you say boo. But if you pretend you're not when you are…. Well you just boo hoo."

With that Harragar rolled about on the grass laughing.

"You are quite mad!"

However, Pretzel was comforted by her odd philosophy. Just a few words from Harragar had given her encouragement for she knew she did not have to pretend to be brave any more.

"Where are your bird friends?"

"Keeping an eye on me up there."

"They'll go with you."

"Of course. They won't abandon me."

Harragar glanced at Pretzel and began to mutter to herself, "How can she know what is in front when she doesn't know .. The Wattoo."

The two meandered home, both deep in their own thoughts, as the wingflits, hidden by the canopy, twittered above. When they reached home Harragar wiped her feet on a tree root and turned.

"Tomorrow we can visit my dell again."

"If I don't leave tomorrow, I never will."

She gave Pretzel a hug. "Then tomorrow I will help you pack and walk with you to the top o the hill."

"But I am following the river."

"Are you stupid or something?"

"It is my flags. I must go that way, but I am really afraid all the same."

"Good, good. That's my gal."

Harragar ladled out the soup and they sat slurping on the back step watching Martha munching contentedly. The sky became a deep blue as the crescent moon began to glisten. It would have been a perfect evening if their hearts weren't so heavy.

They both slept in short spurts until morning when Pretzel woke first and beckoned Roland, who assembled the wingflits at the front entrance.

"We are leaving today at noon."

"Now where!"

Pretzel knew they were delighting in the abundance of berries and would be loathe to be leaving this paradise. She pointed to the mountains while Tachymus shook his head.

"There is danger out there for all of us."

"Then I will have to leave you all here with Harragar"

"We can't let you go without us!"

The young ones twittered excitedly, oblivious to what risks lay ahead.

Harragar appeared at the door.

"I can see your mind is truly made up now and your friends also. Oh, my girl I will miss you, more than I would my goats, my special garden, and my waterfall rides won't ever be the same but I know …this is the way for both of us."

Freya scrutinized Pretzel's face and saw she was fighting her tears but her chin was jutting out determinedly. She was more than aware of her friend's emotional complexities, having watched from her cage Pretzel's grim silence mixed with false humour whenever she was being observed by nurse Barrabesh.

"Keep away from those lanterns if you see them at night. They belong to those mad mud men."

Pretzel remembered the dream she had way back in Grataco. It had warned her about the lights in the hills and now was making sense.

"What if I am seen? What then should I do?"

"You will have to work that out for yourself."

Batwin interrupted crossly, "Lot of help your old mate is now!"

"Manners, Batwin. Wingflits! Fill your beaks with berries for we are travelling on regardless."

Harragar packed together the best portions of her vegetables and fruit, including the green ones to ripen later. She wrapped thick dollops of jam in vine leaves and baked long loaves of sour dough to fill Pretzel's sac to overflowing. When it was time to leave, Harragar walked with her as far as the creek crossing. The two stood arm in arm until the birds became inpatient.

"Harragar, I really do need you. I don't know if I will manage alone."

"Enough of that, my girl. Be off with you now!"

She turned on her heel and after shooing off the wingflits, walked quickly away, pulling out her handkerchief and trying to smother her sobs before turning and giving one quick wave.

*

Drako sat on the school bench chattering with his school mates. Suddenly he felt a sharp pain in his belly and doubled over.

"What's up with you, Drako?"

"I'm not sure. Just a pain in here. Must have been something I ate."

When he returned home he watched closely to see if the worry lines had deepened on his mother's forehead. To his relief it appeared nothing had changed, except that night he could hear her tossing about in her sleep. Next morning dark clouds started to fill the sky.

CHAPTER 12   BUCCASAN

Pretzel stopped several times to catch her last glimpse of Harragar's back receding down the path hoping she might turn round again. She took a deep breath and followed her flags which led her over the hill and into the undergrowth. She pushed her way through thick clumps of ferns that left an itchy substance sticking to her skin. The track passed through numerous fallen tree trunks slippery with moss which she clambered over with care this time, not wanting to repeat another painful landing. Freya remained on Pretzel's shoulder while the rest twittered above, trying not to show impatience with her slow progress as she frequently stopped to scratch her arms and peel away the sap.

"Tell them they must be quiet, Freya."

Freya flew up to one group and then another in an attempt to hush them, but the newer winglets continued to warble excitedly. Eventually she had to call on Tachymus to silence them. The winglets needed frequent reminding for they would forget and begin over again. Pretzel couldn't help smiling, remembering Drako as a baby who wanted to chatter and gurgle until she was driven mad. Baby birds were obviously just the same.

The lower branches, yellow stained with lichen, glowed when shafts of sunlight pierced through the canopy. One would light up, and then another. Despite her qualms at what might lie ahead, Pretzel was struck by the beauty of the forest.

"If it wasn't for those mudmen, I would want to spend more time in this forest, Freya."

"You have to keep going just keep going. I will stay close to you whatever happens."

"Freya, my tiny lifeline! What would I do without you?"

She had heard an occasional sound of rushing water some-where through the trees but now all was quiet except for the croaking of frogs which became louder. She guessed she must have arrived at the swamplands for it was not long before mosquitoes arrived in droves. Pretzel hastily pulled on Reza's pyjamas, slapping at her face but daring not to speak. She fed Freya breadcrumbs before placing the quivering bird alongside her and crawled into her cocoon sac to wait for Roland to report.

"Their nests, I mean huts, are directly across the river as the crows fly," he twittered quietly before flying above.

Darkness fell quickly and Pretzel lay in the pitch blackness seeing in her mind Harragar's brown wrinkled face and kind eyes, feeling a lifetime away from her. This time she felt an extreme pang for Marthamum, Poppo and Drako who would be sitting at the table for dinner. She missed Poppo's strong arms. She had always felt safe with Poppo. And she would never see them again.

"What have I done, Freya? I am now beginning to wonder whether I should have left them."

"In our bird life, we must leave our nests. It is normal for a bird."

"Of course it is, Freya. I must see it your way, mustn't I, that I am simply being normal like a bird with wings."

"A bird with wings," echoed Freya

Pretzel then remembered Harragar's words, "You don't have to pretend you are not scared."

She lay feeing comforted by Freya's presence and had almost dozed off when she heard the sound of men's voices calling to each other. They were bashing their way through the undergrowth towards her. She tried to cover herself with leaves but it was too late. A light lit her up before she could lie down again.

"Ola!"

A man leant down and shone the lantern on her face for what seemed an eternity. His silhouette was broad with square shoulders. 'Not unlike my brother,' she thought briefly, but when he moved the light out of her face and she could see that his hair was caked with mud, his coat consisted of pieces of cloth roughly stitched together and he reeked of that too familiar mud smell, any idea of similarity dissipated.

"I've found a girl!"

He jumped with glee and shouted again but the rest of the group was too busy bashing the trees to hear him. She curled up into her sac knowing it was pointless to try an escape in the darkness and wished she had followed Harragar's advice after all. What would these mudmen do? They harmed her goats, were obviously greedy and violent, and there were no women or girls, in fact no children. She recalled Harragar's tone of voice, "A pretty girl like you." She had learnt that every young girl was safe to wander around her village, but not so in the large cities, but never had she guessed she would have to be wary of a human being in the middle of a forest. 'How stupid and naive I have been,' she thought. Always if caught in the stinging rain on the mountains she could visit a goatherd's enclave and the men there would be as kind and gentle as Poppo. But here this strange man before her was the epitome of Marthamum's cautionary tales of what might befall her if she ever left the village. 'Will he kill me?' These thoughts ran through Pretzel's mind as the man continued to peer into her face. He seemed intrigued by Pretzel's ears, looking at her delicate ones and then rubbing his own. She noticed the axe in his hand, which looked sharp and lethal.

Pretzel had no choice but to resort to manners and try to say as brightly as she could," Hello! I am Pretzel. What is your name?"

He grunted with surprise

"Buccasan."

Pretzel felt for Freya who had nestled deeper into her clothing, knowing the bird would be a mere mouthful if discovered. It would be like chomping down a small nut.

"I'll give you some of my jam if you please leave me alone."

He reached out to feel her bag which was bulging with Harragar's food and she again remembered what Harragar had said about the greed and the laziness of these men. Pretzel had to think quickly for she knew she could not deal with a whole group of them.

"There will be more for you if you don't tell the rest that I am here."

Buccasan put down the lantern and stroked his beard, just like the she had watched the old men in Grataco when deep in thought. He leant forward to explore the contents.

"You give me some, then!"

She wanted to retort," Manners!" but thought it wiser to just hand him some bread and jam which he hungrily devoured.

When the shouts returned Buccasan waved them away, "No tarracoots here," and they disappeared again through the trees.

"Tarracoots?"

"We find them at night. Good. Very good."

He made sucking sounds with his lips.

Pretzel was so grateful that he had diverted the group from stumbling upon her that she did not enquire further.

"Follow me!"

She was heartened by the fact that this strange man was not showing any sign he was intending to kill her. There was no way she could out run him at night, the path being impossible to see. She could either end up in the swamp, or if she tried to escape he might call to the others. His large frame blocked out the light but he turned frequently, shining it onto the logs when they blocked their path. He held out an arm to help her clamber over them which she declined, feeling dismayed that her flags had led her into the company of this foul smelling man. When they arrived at the river, the frogs were deafening as he led her across logs used as stepping stones. She tried to fight off mosquitoes, at the same time using her arms to balance, dreading what lay in that black swamp if she fell. She quickly glanced up at the sky to see a sliver of moon peeping through clouds and cursed under her breath its indifference. At last, with a squelch, Buccasan stepped on to the bank and reached to steady her. This time she did not refuse as the mud gave a sucking sound behind her.

The hut was just visible in the faint moonlight, roughly thrown together, with large gaps in the wood filled up with twigs. There were no windows. Buccasan led her inside and placed his lantern on the ground. The one and only room consisted of a log used as a seat, and a tree trunk used as a table. His bedding on the floor was nothing but a pile of twigs and leaves. To Pretzel's relief, he collapsed onto it and immediately began to snore. She found a grassy bank outside, feeling too exhausted to worry about the next day, and lay watching the moon set. As soon as dawn broke, she explored around her. The river was, as predicted, a murky brown. A rusted pot thick with spider webs lay on its side outside the door of the hut.

Buccasan stepped outside, yawing, and followed her gaze.

"If you clean that, you can cook,"

"I'm not your slave! I am a guest."

"If you feed me I won't hurt you."

"I will do no such thing!"

"Then you're dead!"

"You should be ashamed of yourself, talking to me like that!"

He went to her sac and began to rummage.

"Don't touch my things!"

He stepped back looking crestfallen and gave a smile. She felt sickened by his blackened teeth, yet in the morning light, now that she could see him more clearly, she was surprised to see he was quite young, not much older than herself. He began to hum a sad tune.

"What happened to your family?"

"I was a small boy. I went on a hunt with my father, my older brothers, uncles. Then the earthquake... my pa was killed ... no way home."

He began to sob.

Pretzel could see specks in the sky and guessed they were the wingflits searching for her.

"I am sorry. Until I leave this place I will be your friend, I promise."

"No. Always....you stay with me. I am so lonely. You can be my wife."

Pretzel sighed, for this terrifying hulk of a man had turned into a lost child.

"I will be your sister. Too young to be a wife."

Pretzel realized she was beginning to use Buccasan's manner of speech, then surprised her self by suddenly blurting out, "You get some water from the river and I will wash your hair and beard."

'Oh what have I got myself into now!' she admonished herself.

She remembered how often her mother did that to Poppo, but this... she was shocked that she had volunteered such a thing.

It was as if she had automatically landed in Marthamum's shoes. When he shuffled back she poured the brown water onto his hair and beard which soon became soft, black and glistening. He started to sing as Pretzel felt herself smiling inside, no longer afraid. She felt confused and troubled by that sadness in his eyes as memories of her home crowded in. The flags returned adding to her bewilderment as she heard their whisper of approval.

"I can be a sister for you," Pretzel repeated hopefully.

"Right!"

Pretzel knew she was by no means ready to be anybody's wife despite becoming of age. She had refused to be like her fellow village girls who talked continuously of marriage. At the same time she had never felt like this with Drako. Sisters weren't afraid of their brothers, nor did they feel as if they were disappearing into their eyes. Buccasan sat stroking his beard and watching her. Pretzel turned away and became more business like. She was aware that Harragar's food was fast running out and noted the bones on the ground outside, wondering if they belonged to those tarracoots the men were hunting. She did not fancy them raw whatever they were.

"Now, you can light me a fire and boil up some water."

Buccasan used his flint stones to set the dry leaves alight with ease.

"You can look after yourself better than I can. Why are you so lazy? You can't even speak proper sentences."

Buccasan shrugged his shoulders and looked down at the ground.

"I did not care any more. My two brothers.... taken by the Torpendots."

"What are they?"

"Fierce black animals. In the mountains over there...once pounced on you are dead. They... no chance."

"It must have been so horrible."

"I cry and cry… My mothers and sisters all left behind."

"I am so sorry, Buccasan. What did you all do?"

"The others left here…we fight, catch the tarracoots, sleep until … we wait to die."

"Yet you are all strong enough to steal an old woman's goats."

He shrugged but looked ashamed.

"Why can't you go home?"

Buccasan pointed to the east.

"The torpendots will eat you. No other way to the mountains. Big earthquake changed the land. Big holes. Nowhere to go."

"Then why did the older men not lead you north across the desert?"

"They …some… died in the quicksand and the rest turned back. This no is our home."

Buccasan sat on the ground and rocked back and forth. Pretzel remembered that if it wasn't for Batwin she would have met the same slow and suffocating death, and sat down beside him until he was still. He then turned and looked at her quizzically.

"So where is it your home?"

"A village to the north called Grataco. What the name of your village?"

"Tirracal. It may be buried. It was straight over there."

He pointed in the direction of a ridge that loomed razor sharp in the distance.

"But this now is my home," he repeated, as if trying to convince Pretzel.

"You could build a much better hut away from the bank and mosquitoes. You have an axe and this place stinks. By the way, what are these tarracoots anyway?"

Buccasan pointed to a pile of dead creatures that looked like small mice.

"We swallow them whole."

"Ugh"

"Have one."

"Never never never! I'd vomit! But you can grow things."

She recalled Reza's boys weren't fond of hard work and preferred goat herding to pulling cloth out of the vats, but at least they carted boxes of grapes, fished, and chopped wood.

"Why do you not fish in the river? You can't just live on those ghastly tarracoots."

"We caught them and were poisoned."

"You must have caught the wrong ones. I suspect you come from a place where there are no fish. You have not learnt which are safe to eat. I know how to catch bream. They are tricky to catch as you must play the line, but I will show you how."

Suddenly there was the sound of feet squelching their way up the bank. Pretzel retreated inside Buccasan's hut feeling for Freya who was still deep in her pocket. She heard them greet Buccasan asking why he had returned from the hunt so soon. They reeked of blood and Pretzel had to stop herself from retching. One of the brothers saw the pot and flew into a rage.

"No. No. Mother's and sister's pot. Can't use."

Pretzel heard it being hurled against a tree, and it became clear to her that their brutish ways were an attempt to forget their past and all the maternal comforts it offered. Here in this swamp land, they had chosen to live and die in misery rather than risk returning to nothing.

At last the 'brothers' departed and Pretzel could crawl out and examine the pot for damage.

"Buccasan! I am going to use those tarracoots for bait. Please keep an eye out for your brothers. I know I am not safe in their company, but I am not going to stay like a corpse in your hut for ever."

"They go asleep."

"That's a surprise," muttered Pretzel sarcastically. She could imagine Harragar giving them all a piece of her mind.

Pretzel picked her way along the bank and waited patiently, gradually playing out the line until she pulled in a small bream. She taught Buccasan how to clean and fillet it and together they cooked it, sharing the last of Harragar's bread.

"Listen Buccasan. If only you could befriend that old lady instead of stealing her goats."

"No."

"I think I know. She reminds me of you too much. Is that it?"

He looked down at his hands and nodded silently.

"You must try… She would show you how to grow vegetables and then I would be happy to go on my way."

"You must stay with me."

"I can't."

"I will tell the brothers."

Pretzel decided to bide her time. She waited until the evening when Buccasan curled up to sleep but whenever she tiptoed out he woke instantly with loud yelling and waving. She tried to suppress a giggle as she couldn't help liking his childish ways and despite his bluster and threats, his look of melancholy pulled at her like a magnet. She watched him lying head back, mouth open displaying his crooked teeth. His shoulders moved up and down as he snored. It was not long before he was breathing evenly, and by that time, her desire to escape had faded.

She imagined a mirror. How long ago she had seen herself she did not remember, but instead she saw Buccasan. She closed her eyes, puzzling out this strange condition. This was replaced by a huge gaping hole as her flags were calling, "The Wattoo,

The Wattoo!" Buccasan faded into the background as the distant mountains called and called, but the warm sun, the fish meal, the sound of Buccasan's breathing and the fluttering of Freya close to her lulled her until the darkness of the abyss faded.

A sound made her jump up with a start as a group of men stood at the entrance angrily waving axes above their heads.

CHAPTER 13   THE MUD BROTHERS

The long stems of their axes blocked her path, the metal glinting in the sunlight. Buccasan clambered outside rubbing his eyes.

"Leave that girl alone! She's mine."

The men became more incensed at his protests as they held their axes closer to Pretzel's head. She tried to retreat behind Buccasan but one of the men pushed him away. She wanted to scream but no sound would come out at she felt her tongue dry as a bone. Then she remembered how she had dealt with that first encounter with Buccasan and with as much strength as she could muster, drew herself up to face them.

"My name is Pretzel... I did not mean to intrude... but this kind man helped me when I was lost.... I borrowed your pot to cook my fish and...I will leave straight away truly and excuse me for trespassing for I was lost and are on my way to the mountains and.....what are your names?"

She rambled on not daring to stop as they stared coldly at her, their axes still inches from her face. One man took a step towards her and touched the tip of her nose with his axe. She felt its sharpness and a warm trickle of blood as Buccasan yelped like a dog, throwing himself at him but he was nudged off as if he was an unruly child. Buccasan tried again to wrest an axe from one of them but he was pushed away.

"She is my new sister," he cried but that angered them more.

Pretzel felt as if time had frozen and she was in a dream where all the past had disappeared where the axe handles were like stems floating in a pond. She was looking up from the bottom while above her these grinning faces with their blackened teeth were creatures from another world. She longed for Harragar to be here now. 'She would have known how to deal with them,' she thought, 'Come to think of it, Harragar would have handled them quite differently. I have been far too polite,' so she took a deep breath.

"Now listen, you hopeless ne'er do wells, you goat thieves, you lazy laggards, you dim witted big eared thick brained moth-eaten sons of idiots! Put those axes down!"

The mudmen slowly dropped them. Something in their minds had clicked as they stood open mouthed shaking their heads.

"What do you think you're doing, scaring a visitor like that, you blunt nosed pimply lot of freaks?"

Pretzel surprised herself. She was even enjoying herself, if such a thing was possible with one's life within inches of its disappearance.

"Put them in a pile over there ....the axes stupid!" she said to one that was standing staring at her, his tongue lolling out of his mouth.

"Get them out of Buccasan's doorstep......and sit down the lot of you!"

She wished Harragar was here to approve, for her voice was booming out as if it did not belong to her. As for Drako, he would have been ecstatic. Now that she had their full attention she had to think quickly. She certainly had never had an audience like this before as they sat in front of her wiping the hair out of their eyes to see her better.

"Buccasan told me about you all. He explained how you and your fathers were trapped by the avalanche. I 'm sure that somehow I can help you return to your village but only if you promise not to ever menace me like that again."

One of the men who was bald bar a long piece hair that fell over one shoulder, went to get up. He picked his teeth and then spat on the ground.

"Stop that frightful spitting. Yuk! You make me sick!"

The man with the huge tongue let it loll from his mouth again.

"Shove your tongue back in. You look like a lizard!"

The rest sat looking at her, not daring to grunt, let alone spit.

"It is time you all got yourselves a decent meal for a start. I have a fishing line with me, so you can use those tarracoots for bait. And don't fall asleep! Just wait for the fish to bite and show me you can be of use. I will put this pot on the fire and I don't want to hear a word about not wanting to be reminded of your mothers and all that nonsense!"

Pretzel filled the pot with water while Buccasan looked at her in amazement.

"Sister, sister!"

This gentle little girl had turned into a crabby old woman before his eyes. She had conjured up his past where now he remembered his grandmother who could be bossy also but always with the kindest of eyes. She had grey hair which fell around her shoulders. He then recalled her singing too him but couldn't bear to think any more about it so made himself busy adding sticks to the fire.

'Poor things,' Pretzel thought, 'Sympathy on them is lost. They have never known softness. But Buccasan… he is different.'

She wandered away from the hut to consult her flags and they buzzed with excitement, *"Your escape will be also there's."*

She knew for certain they would continue to guide her. They had led her to Harragar and to this seemingly impossible place despite her first dreadful misgivings, so must trust them.

With Buccasan's instruction, the brothers returned with a bucket load of bream. They watched Pretzel fillet and cook them, soon followed by satisfied slurping and clicking of teeth.

"Try eating with your mouths closed." she laughed, remembering Harragar was also a noisy eater.

"Buccasan, I haven't been introduced yet!"

He at last found his voice.

"This is Mirod, Breg, Fallat, Pinto, Vroog, Sennotan, Gugat and Tosh."

"I'll try to say them. Mirod, Greg, Vrog, Tosh....I will learn...Now ...do you all want to return to your village or remain here till you forget all about it and I also will leave you here."

Buccasan looked horrified.

"You...not go now." Mirod cried, shaking his head until pieces of mud flew around Pretzel.

"Ah, one of you has a voice. "

"You will really help us go home?"

Mirod smoothed his matted hair down in attempt to look more presentable. Pretzel had to think fast. She felt for Freya who all this time had been nestled quietly in her pocket and whispered to her, "Freya! I have thought of something."

Tosh, the one with the drooling tongue, looked at her with surprise to see Pretzel talking to her pocket, but she figured she had shocked them all enough to know that anything was possible. However, she needed time to herself to think. How could she convince them that a little edible bird could be helpful? Then she thought again, 'Why? They needn't know anything about the wingflits.'

"Freya. I must speak with Batwin. Fly off with speed and they won't catch you."

She lifted Freya out and threw her into the air.

Mirod gasped, "You a magician!"

"Now it is time for you to return to your huts."

This time Pretzel was grateful for their lassitude as she needed time. She made her way along the river bank until well out of sight where Batwin and Freya flew down, Batwin giving a gentle peck of greeting.

"I expect you may not like this idea but please trust me."

"What is that? I thought we were no longer in need of any more of your ideas."

"Well there is another one. I hope this will be the last... I need another topaz."

Batwin flapped his wings furiously.

"No!"

"Not to," added Freya.

"I will never forget that it saved my life ...twice."

Batwin looked unconvinced.

"I will write to Harragar, and when she receives this note, she will give you her special berries."

Pretzel felt fleetingly guilty at bribing Batwin, but she had seen that Batwin was a brave bird who loved challenges and was easily bored if nothing exciting happened. She suspected that already he was tired of waiting for her and would have mooched about in those trees. And then there was Freya. Freya was obviously impressed with Batwin's courage, while he seemed more than fond of Freya.

He puffed himself up.

"My mind is made up. I will fly and hurry back with..."

"Wait till I write this."

Pretzel quickly jotted a note on a crumpled sheet of paper, "Dear Harragar, please give Batwin your berries for I have promised them to him. The mudmen will follow later and will not steal your goats Please can you supply them with potatoes and leeks, then ferry them over the river. I am safe, love Pretzel."

There was no room to write anymore. She guessed Harragar would understand and not think she had gone totally out of her mind.

Batwin took it in his beak and flew off down the river.

"Tell the others, Freya, to be patient. Stay with them now for my pocket is not a place for a little free flying bird."

"I will stay with you."

"Now that you have been spotted, it is far too dangerous."

Freya's feathers were looking somewhat disheveled after days of being cramped. After preening herself, she flew a circle of farewell. Pretzel watched her greet the others as the specks in the sky formed the familiar zigzag pattern.

She knew it would be many long days of waiting for Batwin's return. She wandered well away from the river using the Goplin Thirkins to orientate her, and discovered a tall tree that had crimson fruit hanging from high branches. Thorns sprouted from them in the places where she need to take a hold and she ripped her hands which bled over the fruit she retrieved, but the delicious taste was worth the effort. She brought them back for Buccasan to share with the brothers.

"You all need nourishment," she explained." Now see what you can find here if you look!"

Next morning she explored up river to where it narrowed. She was about to wash her clothes in it but Mirod followed her calling out to come back. She then saw what he was pointing to. There were large paw prints in the sand. She thanked him but still could not trust him so brushed quickly past him, returning to the hut of Buccasan.

"You are different from the others."

"They are all brothers to me now. They all I have."

"Do you remember more than them? Is that why you are kind? "

"I remember."

He hummed quietly as his eyes softened.

"My grandmother's song."

"Do you know the words?"

"Baby jewel of the night.....sleep under the moon so bright....all the world's a ...silent place, when your nonna ... strokes your face."

Tears welled up in his eyes, "Will we really go home?"

"I am working on a plan, but please, no more questions."

Pretzel could think of nothing worse than to raise their hopes, and then dash them if Batwin did not return. She also wondered if there was any village to return to, but they had to find that out for themselves. She had in time softened her attitude to them, now knowing their anguish. Weeks passed by as Pretzel tried hard not to show her anxiety for Batwin which they knew nothing about. She had to keep reassuring them that it was taking all this time to think what to do. At times she could make out Freya perched alone on a branch, and felt sick at the thought if she was the cause of Batwin's demise. She spent her days fishing, or wandering into the forest, and made up songs to Buccasan's tunes but at night she would lie awake trembling, knowing she would never forgive herself if Batwin did not return and knowing if that was the case she would leave on her own ashamed at letting down the wingflits so badly.

At last a night came when she dreamt of her brother. He was walking on the road to school, kicking pebbles in his usual way but then it changed to his returning home where he was lifting back P. D.s fur to admire the five red stones that remained. He made a start as a bird landed on the floor and neatly picked out another before flying off. The dream put her in a lighter mood but she continued to worry nevertheless, until one morning she woke to find a topaz glowing red in her palm. She raced out of the hut to see the wingflits flying in a circle of greeting to meet Batwin and sobbed with relief.

"Buccasan! It is time for a meeting."

When all the brothers had been rounded up outside Buccasan's hut, Pretzel waited until she had their full attention which seemed an age as Mirod was concentrating more on the wart on his ankle.

"You can now return to your village in the mountains, to the home of your mothers and fathers"

Vroog thumped his head and began to sob.

"You will cross the swamp and follow the path, which you well know, to the old lady whose name is Harragar. It is your job to reassure her you will not be stealing her goats and you must talk politely to her with no spitting or suchlike. You will not need all your axes as that will frighten her. Only Buccasan will carry one for he is your leader now."

"My sister! You are coming too?"

"I am continuing south."

"The torpendots will eat you!

"I will just have to find a safe way round them."

"You cannot leave me now."

Pretzel felt her heart tearing apart. How much she had learned to love him beyond anything she had felt before, but the pull of the Wattoo was strong as she released his grasp.

"It is too much to ask for you to understand, but you won't ever forget me, will you Buccasan?"

"We go now," called Tosh.

"I haven't finished. Harragar will give you potatoes, berries and bread. She may even give you her precious jam if you climb her ladder and collect more berries for her. She will take you across the river on her mattress and there you will see a path leading north. You will eventually arrive at a tall city from which you will smell delicious aromas of soup, or baking of bread. You must not enter the city even if your bellies ache. You must listen to what I say. Buccasan, do not let your brothers through those gates. Instead you will make do with the fruits of the desert, the Catoa. There will be plenty enough to keep your bellies satisfied. Somewhere in the middle of the desert you will find fields of wonderful colours. Throw them some of your Catoa and stay on the path. If one of you steps on the yellow sand, which is quicksand, this stone will pull you free."

Pretzel handed the stone to Buccasan while the rest crowded around it grunting with delight.

"You must take great care of it for it will save you from a terrible death. On the other side of the desert you must follow the cliffs and continue northward. You will come to a large rock with a slit in it. It is there that you must pass silently. Not a grunt from you Tosh or anyone of you. There is an angry and hungry creature living inside it. You will need to practice being quiet, so no lip smacking, Tosh."

Tosh smacked his lips.

"Yes, get it out of your systems now."

They all laughed and gave snorts and whoops until Pretzel silenced them again.

"You will arrive at a lake with a village on the hill. When you see a boy with a dog, address him as Drako and tell him his sister is safe but there is more she must do. He must explain this to my mother. He will show you the path to Tirracal through the northern pass. "

There were tears in the men's eyes.

"Your mother? You have a mother!"

By this tine Tosh was sniveling into his elbow, and Mirod was hiccoughing while Vroog rocked back and forth. Pinto stared ahead of him and bit his lip, but Buccasan was silent, for he was battling his own dilemma. How much he wanted to follow Pretzel, but the call of his village caused him to stand tongue tied.

"It is time to pack together your belongings, Buccasan."

The sun was sinking fast and the mudmen were keen to be on their way. Pretzel took Buccasan by the hand and led him to the edge of the swamp.

"I am not leaving you."

"You must."

The men made their way over the logs and stopped to wait for Buccasan before continuing on He listened to them calling to each other from the other side until their voices faded away. It was only then he jumped off the bank on to the logs to follow them without looking back.

The sound of the wind in the trees reminded Pretzel she was alone again as she walked slowly back to the hut.

CHAPTER 14   THE TORPENDOTS

Pretzel remained outside the hut watching the sun set behind the western peaks, feeling as if her heart was sinking with it. She had half wished that Buccasan would appear out of the twilight, already missing his melancholy expression that would transform into a shy smile when he looked at her. She sat in the darkness willing the moon to rise, the deepness of the night made worse by the distant howls of the torpendots. Somewhere out there the wingflits had nested. She couldn't help feeling a pang of jealousy.

"I never thought I would ever be jealous of a bird, but the truth is I am. They just live and squabble and make up but stay together," but then she reminded herself that it was she who had chosen her exile and she only had herself to blame..

"No one has sent me away from Grataco. It was of my own volition, so why am I so upset?"

She was aware of her flags waving above her reverently as if they understood her state of mind.

"Oh flags. This is all too hard. I am really homesick. I never thought I would admit it but I am."

"Then you know what to do. Turn back if you want!"

"Oh Yes! And abandon the Wattoo?"

"You could you know, before it is too late."

"But it is calling me."

"We know that only too well now."

She tried to sleep but tossed and turned, but at the first glimmer of light she jumped up with excitement. The sun shone directly onto a peak in the distance turning it gold and she knew in her bones that it had to be Mt Vordak. The flags formed a distinct V shape and pointed directly in that direction. By the time the sun had warmed the hut she could not wait to meet up with the wingflits, and wondered why they had not flown down to wake her until she saw an eagle circling above. The birds had waited for what seemed an eternity before they felt safe to fly down and made a huge commotion as their long wait was soon to change.

"You all wish to travel further with me?"

Tachymus nodded his head solemnly, "We will see."

"You know I will stay with you," added Freya.

Now that Pretzel felt her sense of adventure resume in earnest, she wondered how she could have even considered retracing her steps. She would never have forgiven herself.

All day she tore her arms to shreds gathering the fruit from the thorn bushes. She ground down the remaining fish into a paste before filling her bottles with the muddied water, hoping she would find clearer running streams in this unknown land. The image of those soft eyes of Buccasan unnerved her and she tried to put him out of her mind as she packed her sac to the brim. When evening came the peaks were bathed in crimson light as if welcoming her but next morning Roland appeared.

"Big cats. Too many."

"The men call them torpendots. That is the reason they could not return home, but I'll have to see for me- I mean my self. My flags are telling me to go this way and those old flags can't be wrong! Oh! I am sounding like Harragar...and I'm trying to be brave!"

"Stay with you," Freya chirped.

"No, you must keep to the shrubs and ledges away from the eagles, Freya."

Pretzel waded along the river for what seemed hours until it reached a deep gorge where beyond she could see clearly row upon row of sharp peaks, the furthermost taller than the ones in front. They looked like an impenetrable wall. Once she had seen a drawing of their pointed shapes which reminded her of a geography class at school.

"I am going to meet them come what may!"

She clambered on to a rocky outcrop to get her bearings. Suddenly Roland reappeared flapping his wings in frenzy. A group of black specks were at the far end of the valley and moving in her direction. She looked above her at the towering cliffs desperately searching for a foothold. As they came closer she could make out their massive bear like bodies and wide paws that could balance on the moving shale of rock which rolled away from them like numerous small landslides with each step. She could now she that the adults were pitch black while the younger ones were reddish brown. They all had white spots on their feet. They stopped to sniff the air and the leader gave a massive howl that echoed round the cliffs. Pretzel picked her way along the ridge, shaking with fear until at last she found a foot hold up a rock face which she hoped was too sheer for them to climb. There was a cave which at least gave her safety for the night but there was no way she could sleep with the howls echoing below. The birds joined her and huddled together at the back of the cave, remaining deathly silent but for the occasional flap of wings when they changed places.

As soon as it was daylight Pretzel crawled out to look at the river far below, a thin ribbon of brown mixed with streaks of startling blue where the water from the higher peaks intermingled. A low rumbling growl came from the pack of torpendots waiting below. Pretzel had to move on regardless, so grabbed her sac and headed onto the scree. As soon as they saw her, they began pursuit and she climbed with as much speed as she could muster in the higher altitude feeling as if her heart would give out from exhaustion. As she continued to climb, stones rained onto them which had no effect in slowing them down. A small cub caught up with her and snapped at her feet. She kicked it away but it immediately recovered and continued after her. With all her might, Pretzel rolled a rock onto its path making it lose balance and disappear over the edge, howling as it plummeted down the side. At last she reached another rocky outcrop where she could climb out of their reach and gather her strength before the next dash along the scree. She was terrified that night would fall before she could find shelter, but to her relief the torpendots eventually tired before she had, and stood for a while sniffing the air until the leader turned around leading them back down to the valley.

Pretzel made her way carefully along another razor sharp ridge and stopped only when she was satisfied she was safely out of range. She now had a clear view of the eastern ranges and could see where the mud men had been trapped by the rock fall, for their only way back would have been via the gorge. She felt sickened at how they had lost their lives, either from the avalanche itself or having been attacked and eaten. When she rounded the last pinnacle of rock, she had an unimpeded view of Mt Vordak which loomed like a sentry. The light was so much cleaner and brighter in these high peaks and she was enchanted by the view and could have stayed all day but for the fact she would not want to remain here to sleep on the mountain side with the whole world sliding away beneath her. She had to move fast.

"Roland! I will need you to find the best way down."

"There is no shelter here from the eagles. You haven't thought of us."

"I'm sorry. The last thing I intend is to put you all in danger on my account, but…I have an idea. Why not all of you stay close to me, and if I wave these pyjamas I can ward off any eagles."

Sorro spun and somersaulted with glee as she pulled them from her sac.

"I will continue to wave these until we get to the bottom. That river must be Upper Banzoor and I can see there are trees lining the banks where there will be good nesting places."

Roland flew on ahead to scout.

"Come back Roland.' chirped Tachymus. "Pretzel is right. She can protect us."

There was a muttering and twittering from some of the birds,"Oh here this girl goes again," who were remembering their safe nests upriver in the large pines, but Pretzel guessed the wingflits, even Batwin, were enjoying this adventure, and the subsequent stories that would be handed down from winglet to winglet for ever more. As for Freya, she was always devoted to Pretzel's safety while Pretzel now guessed that Batwin would never leave Freya. It was a joyous bunch that moved along the ridge with Pretzel stopping frequently to wave her pyjamas at the eagles that circled above them in the cloudless sky.

"This would be quite a picnic if I wasn't over eight thousand feet up. Remember to show me where I can find a footing. I can't fly!"

Roland put his head to one side to view her sympathetically as Pretzel gritted her teeth. Poppo had taught her the rule of rock climbing. Never put one foot into a new place without being supported with the foot behind. Make sure the handholds are secure, and never clutch at a plant in case it pulls away. In any case this terrain was far too crumbly for most plants to survive against the massive downpours of rain in winter. Pretzel had been good with heights as a child, but never had she been on rocks like this that slipped and rolled away from her with each step.

"Not that not that." Roland called out frequently, as she inched her way down the mountain side. When she stopped to draw breath, her legs shook uncontrollably.

"Halfway," chirped Freya.

The trees began to take shape. When tufts of grass peeped out of the shale, Pretzel knew she was safe to stand and step from rock to rock until at last she could slither down on the gravel to reach the river. By this time the wingflits were free to fly on ahead and by the time she caught up with them they were dipping and diving and spraying cool water over her. She was too exhausted to join in the fun and collapsed into her sac. She lay looking up at Mount Vordak which she could now see was totally bare and absent of caves. The next part of her journey would have to be alone. Again she was overcome with apprehension and in the night Freya flew down beside her, drying Pretzel's forehead with her wing when she became drenched in sweat.

Next morning, Sorro flew in and out of the trees with delighted squawks while Tachymus nodded approvingly for he knew Sorro was a useful diversion for the winglets. They were all fond of this strange human - girl, who had made up her mind to climb that fearful mountain on her own.

Pretzel gazed up at the sky which was bluer than she had seen in her life, reminding her of the colour of Reza's silk, or of Drako's eyes in late afternoon. There was not a tuft of cloud to be seen, just the bright morning sun already burning into her scarf.

"You all must know I have to say good bye."

Tachymus tried half heartedly to dissuade her but remembered too well that first encounter by the lake, the swirling colours that had materialized from the water after she threw in the

Topaz and knew that there was no way now she would change her mind. The wingflits could not argue with Tachymus who knew already their beloved Pretzel was well on her way to meeting the Wattoo.

"Can we come some of the way?" the winglets asked excitedly.

"No point."

Tachymus gathered them all together for the farewell parting with wing feather kisses. Pretzel watched them flying in their zigzag style as the sky dissolved in her tears.

*

Harragar was up at dawn milking her goats, feeling bemused at that last encounter with the mudmen. They had kept to Pretzel's promise of not harming her or her goats, but she was happy she had her house back to herself again, for they snorted all the time and smacked their lips, particularly the one with the large tongue.

As the day wore on, her old hands began to tremble, and by nightfall she had no appetite She woke listening to the wind outside, reminding her of the winds that had whistled around her on that mountain all those years ago.

*

Drako kept staring out of the window of the classroom and noted the sky was an unusual iridescent blue. It was as though he was looking into a deep pool of infinity and it unnerved him. He put is head in his hands.

"You do not seem well, Drako. I think you should go home."

Drako gratefully picked up his satchel, and as soon as he was out of sight, ran up the hill until he could run no more. When he stopped, his legs shook uncontrollably.

CHAPTER 15   MOUNT VORDAK

Pretzel watched her companions become mere specks in the sky and felt numb.

"There was so little time to say a proper goodbye and now they are gone."

"And don't we count for anything?"

"I know you do but it is just not the same. You are …all too serious I suppose."

"How else will you listen to us?"

She sighed and looked up at the summit. She could see that the first part was comparatively easy as a trail of rocks led up to a ridge, but from there the scree would test her endurance. This carried on up to a steep cliff reaching to the peak.

She felt tired but there was nothing she could do but start her climb over the rocks and when she reached the ridge she was able to rest. She looked down at a deep gully with sparse trees gently waving in the breeze and inched her way round the ridge where the wind met her from the western side. She would have liked to remain here enjoying the coolness but her flags were impatient for her to move on up the scree.

She had only climbed about another fifty metres when a sudden movement caught her eye, followed by a feather light touch on her shoulder which stopped her in her tracks.

"Freya!"

"Who else, Pretzi?"

"This is far too dangerous for a small bird like you. You shouldn't have left the flock. "

"You saved my life, remember and I couldn't leave you to be alone now."

Pretzel felt overjoyed despite her concern for Freya's safety.

"'You brave and foolhardy little bird! ... But what about Batwin? He must have tried to stop you."

Freya put her head under her wing for a moment before chirping softly.

"He was cross with me. So cross when I told him I was turning around."

"Oh, Freya!"

Pretzel stroked Freya's head.

"You will meet up with him again... but he must be terrified for you. Promise to stay close to me and I can shelter you from the eagles. I will never forgive myself if something happens to you."

"My life. My life."

"Yes. I know it is your choice but if you had not met me..."

"I would be still in that cage or dead."

They continued up the slope together, with frequent stops for Pretzel to get her breath back due to the thin mountain air. The Goplin Thirkins were bathed in sunlight contrasting with their deep gullies. She could now see more clearly their pointed shapes going on for ever. It seemed that the only mountain that had a flattened area on the top was this one. She was high enough now to see that the River Banzoor was met by a striking blue stream pouring from the glaciers on the distant mountains and would have given anything to splash her face in it but there was no stream on bare Mt. Vordak, just the occasional trapped puddle of water. Freya stayed close, darting frequently out from the protection of Pretzel's sac to feed on small flying insects. When they arrived at an overhang Pretzel stopped.

"It doesn't look that there will be any further shelter after here, Freya."

Pretzel looked up at her flags which seemed transparent in the rarified air and felt a lump in her throat as she stroked a farewell to Freya who she could see was determined to wait for her.

She carried on, the afternoon sun beating down as her steps became more laboured in the higher altitude. When she stopped to catch her breath, she noticed a fat brown lizard sunning itself on the rocks, displaying its darting tongue, but eventually all life seemed to vanish. Night came swiftly and she huddled in a small gully out of the wind. There was no moon yet to comfort her, but instead the sky was brilliant with stars. She felt if she reached out her hand she could touch them. She lay chilled to the bone but eventually managed to sleep. She dreamt of Harragar ladling out those familiar beans floating in thick lumps of gravy. She was calling out, "Good for you gal. You are meeting the Wattoo."

When Pretzel woke, the summit was veiled in dawn mist. She looked down and called to Freya in the hope she might hear her, and thought she heard a chirp coming from far below.

It was time to make for the top. It seemed such a short distance but appeared to become further away each step she took and her knees were aching by the time she arrived at the cliff face. Now she had to gather her strength as well as scrutinize it for possible footholds. Her flags waved encouragingly as she began to inch herself up the cliff face and was glad of what appeared a succession of firm handholds that did not pull away as the scree had done. When she looked down she could see the overhang where she had left Freya but felt immediately dizzy so pulled herself to the top of the cliff. To her astonishment what now lay before her was a crater tucked in beneath the peak. As she slid towards it, the edges crumbled away, so on the opposite side found a firm ledge that she could lean over to explore. Masses of vines reached up from the darkness, and attached to them were clusters of tangerine fruit that resembled large grapes. The sun appeared from behind a cloud turning the vines a brilliant green. She wedged her feet into a crack and reached for the closest fruit. It had a peach like aroma and she tasted it appreciatively before eating half and throwing the rest of it down in Freya's direction.

"An odd way to share breakfast," she exclaimed to her flags that fluttered above her but remained silent as if expectant of her next move.

Pretzel hadn't realized how hungry she was after her diet of dried fish and reached out for another fruit, but this time she lost her grip on the rock and slithered down. She grabbed an armful of vine and with a desperate effort she hung on and pulled herself back up, mashing the vine stem into a pulp. The inside core was like a thick cord strong enough to hold her and after she dragged herself back up on to the rim she lay with her heart beating in her throat as the vines swung into nothingness below.

Harragar's instructions now began to make sense, 'Whatever you do, don't fall. You must jump.'

That was all she could get out of Harragar at that time and those questions she had asked were just followed by a 'yes' or a laugh or a "You will understand." It was frustrating, but now as she faced the Wattoo she had found the solution to Harragar's strange riddle which did not help at all. It just made her more terrified.

"Surely she doesn't mean me to die! This can't be true that I just jump in to this empty space!"

The flags waved above her.

"Listen to Harragar. She said you must not fall. Keep watching the Wattoo and when you are ready, leap!"

She stared down into the darkness. The more terrified she felt, the blacker it appeared even now that the sun was high above her. She pictured Tachymus giving her a memorial service. He would be reading words from a leaf as the others sat in a semicircle, their beaks pointing to the ground. 'This is to commemorate a brave little lady called Pretzel. She left her home in the hills to follow her path through deserts, terrifying cities, swollen brown rivers and wild men with axes. She tramped on to her destiny, losing her life on the Great Mount Vordak. We will never forget our tall legged companion. Each bird would then pull out soft leaves from under their wings to dab their eyes, before flying in a zed formation, paying homage to their long lost friend. Her story would become legend to the winglets when they hatch in the spring, and over time it would change as legends do, as the original wingflits would fall one by one out of the sky. Pretzel could not bear to think of it.

She switched her thoughts to Marthamum and Poppo, sitting under an olive tree in the midday sun, munching potato cakes washed down with wine water. Drako will be at school playing marbles in the square, his possum dog faithfully waiting outside the grounds. As for Buccasan, he will be well on his way home. She imagined his home coming. The village which she hoped desperately was still in existence, would be celebrating the news of their imminent arrival. And Freya! She was sick to the heart wondering how long Freya would wait for her, before sadly rejoining her beloved Batwin.

She looked up again at her flags and made a move toward the edge. As she stared down into the hole, to her surprise the blackness disappeared to be replaced by a mass of swirling colours, just like the time she had looked into Lake Grataco when she threw in the topaz all those months ago. Pretzel took a deep breath, holding her nose automatically as if jumping into a pool and after several attempts at to-ing and fro-ing, leapt.

The air felt chill as she fell past vines flashing deeper green, purple, dark brown and black until there was barely light at all to see, but as soon as it was completely dark she felt the vines leaning out to hold her and break her fall. She looked around her with awe as their tendrils reached out to support her. They appeared lit up from inside them as they glowed with a yellow light which faded the further she fell. By the time she had almost slowed to a halt the light disappeared and with a gentle hiccough, she landed on firm ground, her legs crumpling slowly beneath her.

When she regained her balance she felt around the base which led into a cave. Above her the sky was just a small ring of blue. She heard water trickling through the rocks, and reached her hand out to splash her face in the cold stream that disappeared into the depths of the mountain.

Suddenly flashes of light came from some of the pebbles beneath her feet. She groped for one and picked it up, feeling its smoothness from being worn by the constant flow of water. After holding it in her palm for some time it was warmed by her hands and then to her astonishment the whole pebble became translucent with the light emanating from a tiny insect inside. The pebble then opened up, releasing the insect which flew around her and to her astonishment she immediately could see Reza's silk, which then changed into balloons bobbing from poles in the market square, pearl shells, black horses riding off into a brilliant blue sky. There were trees she had never seen before festooned with lizards whose skin glowed under a cascade of what appeared like the tiniest of moons. Her images became more and more bizarre and seemed endless until she caught the fly which reinserted itself back into the pebble, when the visions disappeared.

Now Pretzel could make sense of those words of Harragar, the whisperings in her sleep with the smile on her lips. Pretzel would never have thought she had come all this way to find a few extraordinary pebbles. But here she sat feeling opened up like a book that she had never read before. She wanted to stay here forever, gathering up as many pebbles as she could, filling her pockets and her cocoon sac, and opening one after the other, as each time a new picture appeared. From another pebble she could hear a melody coming from a shell like structure and which gave out such haunting sounds she wanted to cry for they spoke to her of another time past or future she could not tell. Not all the images were to her liking and some were deeply disturbing, but all were different and exciting none the less.

She wanted to race back to Harragar, revealing her find, but that was tomorrow's problem. The circle of blue above her faded into night and replaced by a cluster of stars shining brilliant as diamonds. She chose not to be concerned at the moment for here she had arrived, and with the encouragement of Harragar, had faced this leap alone into the blackness. She now had no intention of leaving this wondrous place. She was surrounded by an abundance of the grapelike fruit that dropped off the vines to the crater floor, there was fresh water ice cool and sweet which trickled from the depths of Mt Vordak. No longer did the blackness terrify her. She leant against the wall of rock as if it was a comfortable cushion to sleep, but when she awoke, when the small circle above her changed to the grey of dawn, she remembered her little friend Freya waiting alone on that terrifying mountain.

CHAPTER 16   THE WATTOO

The night seemed endless until the morning light appeared over the top of the Wattoo. There was a faint glimmer of the vines above as Pretzel waited for the sun to appear. For a brief moment when it was directly above, the vines lit up a brilliant green and only then she could see where they sprouted from gaps in the rock well beyond her reach. She hoped she would be able to make out a foothold up to their stems and from there she could climb up to the top. The trouble was that where she was sitting she was in deep shadow. She tried to picture the rocks in her mind, imagining there may be places she could hang onto and feel her way up. The climb would have to be done with speed for there would be no chance of rest and she would certainly fall to her death if night fell.

She crawled alongside the stream which trickled its way to the end of the cave before disappearing into the blackness. She had considered she might follow it through the rocks, but the risk was too great. One slip and she could be dragged with the current into the bowels of Mount Vordak. The only way out was to go up the way she came, but she was puzzled how Harragar had managed to return home all those years ago. She was aware of her flags giving her the impression they had all the time in the world as she asked them again and again what she must do. Their nonchalance was aggravating.

"You will see when the time comes," was all she could extract from them.

The Wattoo had given her support when she fell, water to drink, fruit that fell from the vines above and wondrous pebbles that allowed her to see the world in an endless variety of ways but they were not showing her a way out either. She asked herself, 'Do I just sit here passively and be patient? It is no good screaming for help. No person travels this way.' The only hope she had was to hang onto Harragar's frequent comments, "Wait, my girl. You will find out more in due course."

*

Freya pecked disconsolately at the insects around her. At night she listened to the occasional distant roar of a Torpendot and waited for the dawn when she could at least play with the feathery shadows made by her wings, seek water in the crevices, and look hopefully up at the summit where she had last seen her companion disappear over the edge. One morning, when beginning to wonder how long she should wait for Pretzel before assuming she was lost, she saw a speck coming towards her and hid well beneath an overhang, but to her astonishment it was Batwin who landed beside her, his domed beak glistening in the morning sun.

"Freya, you are alive!"

He placed his beak against hers in relief.

"What a stubborn bird you have been."

"Our friend is on the top of the mountain and has not come down."

"Then sadly she is dead, for she would not have left you here all alone."

"We can't just fly away and leave her."

"The winter snows will soon be upon us and then we'll both freeze and drop out of the sky."

"Not yet!"

Batwin bobbed his head up and down in exasperation.

"My sweet and precious Freya! I have risked being eagle food in order to be with you again."

"I <u>must</u> wait for Pretzel. We need more time. Please. "

"I am afraid our dear friend wouldn't listen to anyone but the old witch. Why doesn't she help her? She's a witch and in any case she was the one who instructed to go up the mountain."

"You know you all told her to meet the Wattoo. It was nothing to do with me as I was not with you then and you gave her the topaz to throw in to the Lake. You told all this to me, Batwin, and so it was you that got her into this place and now you think it is all her fault so…well that's that and I am not going from this place till she returns."

"Then we will both die here, the both of us."

"You have known all along she was fated to find the Wattoo. So it was you all that started it. And you all feasted on Harragar's berries and the old lady didn't chase you away. Then we all traveled with our friend to this unspeakable mountain where I can't find a twitter of a word to describe how it must be for a creature without wings to venture to this place. And have you forgotten already that she saved me from dying of thirst and starvation and bird sadness which is the worst of all when birds are forced into cages? We can't fly just away now and leave her."

They both remained huddled under the rocks in silence listening to the mournful cries of the torpendots.

"I will go and look for her."

"I promised with my claw on my chest I would stay here and not follow her."

"I didn't promise her anything. I will fly up when the eagles are asleep."

"The night creatures may take you."

Batwin was determined to investigate as it was the only chance he had to convince Freya to turn back. The next night was lit up by a half moon when Batwin took off up the mountain and found to his alarm that the Wattoo legend was worse than her had thought He had imagined a tiny mountain lake but instead an ominous black hole. There were no swirling colours as had appeared in Lake Grataco and he felt sick to the heart as he perched waiting until a shaft of light entered it but there was no chance of it shining onto Pretzel. As the moon set in the west he continued to perch and think until he made up his mind.

"I led her into this and I have to find some way of knowing if she is still alive."

He flew back to join a quivering Freya who had not had a minute's sleep.

"You are right, Freya. She is all alone down there. We have to think."

"I have been thinking…I feel it in my feathers that is what she needs right now."

"What?"

"Another topaz."

"But what if she is dead? How will we know and then what would be the use of it?"

"I would know if she was dead. I would feel it in my feathers, and I also know she needs us now, Batwin. And I also know another thing. You love this foolhardy human girl as much as I."

"Then come with me, Freya.. We can pick out another stone together."

"You will be faster if you go alone. I will wait here."

There was no point in arguing the point any further as yet again Batwin had to part with Freya, flying his zigzag flight before disappearing into the sky.

*

Meanwhile, the longer Pretzel remained, the more enchanted she came with the pebbles of the Wattoo which she broke open over and over again. Despite the monotony of her fruit diet as they continued to drop from the vines, she felt content, exercising her legs by day and at night waiting for the moon to briefly shine down onto the vines, but in the deepest of night she worried herself sick about her little friend waiting above and knew she would rather die rather than abandon her. How she longed to be stroking Freya's downy feathers as before and had to keep reminding herself that had she not embarked on this seemingly foolhardy adventure, Freya would still be a prisoner in that unspeakable hospital.

*

One night, Drako woke with a start at the sound of tapping. By the time his eyes were accustomed to the darkness all was quiet. He automatically felt for his dog and turned on the light and to his consternation another stone had vanished.

"Now there are only three left."

He made his way outside to find the thief, but there was not a sign of anyone and returned to lie and grieve. Next morning he looked out to see that the sun shone onto a green feather lying on the window sill. He felt bemusement now that the criminal was definitely a bird, but all the same felt he needed to lock the window at night just in case it would return. and take another.

*

Pretzel began to notice that the amount of fruit that fell from the vines was diminishing quite fast. She wondered what Freya would be doing now. Would she fly back to Harragar to ask her to bring a strong rope? But then she remembered the old lady would not be strong enough for the journey so there would be little point in trying that. She dared not lose heart for that would be the end of her. All the same, she began to feel angry with Harragar. Angry that she hadn't warned her that to meet the Wattoo was well and good, but to leave it: that was another story.

One morning, she woke up no longer wanting her pebbles for entertainment and began to feel even more desperate. She heard a sound from what could have been a coin pinging from one wall to the other until an object landed at her feet. She felt for it and picked it up to see a red glow that became bright enough for her to make out her fingers clearly and soon recognized it as a topaz, this one large enough to hold firmly in her hand. When she held it above her it shone on to small crevices which crossed diagonally up the rock face towards the sturdy stem of a vine. She looked up at the ring of blue to see two specks circling before disappearing from sight as she held the stone to her chest and cried.

She hurriedly collected as many pebbles she could carry in her sac, and with one hand gripping the topaz to light her way, began to climb. After she groped her way up to the vines, she slowly hoisted herself up to the top, her arms aching and by the time she was over the rim, she lay there exhausted but was able to hold up the topaz and signal weakly in the direction of the overhang below. It was only then she saw her flags waving at her approvingly.

"So! What would have I done without Batwin to help me? You would have let me stay there and die."\

"*You would have seen the way when you gave your pebbles a break.*"

"Nonsense!"

"*You were too entranced with them to see any light.*"

"But surely not!"

She broke one open which revealed images swirling by of Harragar's house in the rock, of Marthamum knitting leggings by the fire, of large walls hiding short Saraden men, and then the deep brown eyes of Buccasan and suddenly now she was out of danger, felt acutely the sadness of his parting.

"I have these. And now I am out of danger, what now, flags? I don't need you any more for I'm tired of your riddles!"

When she returned the pebble to her sac she became aware of her flags dancing around the rim of the Wattoo and waving farewell.

"No way could my pebbles put me in danger!"

It was time to leave the peak. She slithered down to meet Batwin and Freya who fluttered around her with joy. She started to follow them down the mountain but felt the topaz in her pocket becoming heavier with each step. She sensed that it was reluctant to leave the peak and despite an exclamation form Batwin, she scrambled back up again to the Wattoo. She stood at the rim and threw the topaz over the edge before she could change her mind. When she peered over the edge there was a red glow in the depths and round it danced the flags, this time no longer aware of her.

CHAPTER 17   THE BILLOWS

Pretzel lowered herself gingerly into the River Banzoor. It was so much colder than on the day she had left to climb the mountain. The trees were losing their leaves and soon would have no protection for her gallant companions. Batwin and Freya preened their feathers in the branches above and watched as she clambered out before laying out the fruit in the sun to dry. The small green ones would slowly ripen over the coming weeks.

"As I don't know what they are called, I am naming them 'Pomoka', for they are the colour of pomegranate, as luscious as tomatoes, and my saviours just as the Catoa were in the desert."

"Pomoka, pomoka," chirped Freya, who flew down to investigate.

Pretzel scrutinized the ridge. She thought she might follow it the way she came, this time staying high to avoid the torpendots, but she could see that already ice was forming on the top and it was now impossible. She had dreamt of racing down the hill and surprising Harragar with gleeful stories of her adventures, showing her the Vordak pebbles while savouring her wonderful soups again, but now she was forced to go another way with this time no longer having her flags to guide her. She tried to shrug off her feelings of loss as now she had to make up her own mind where she would go. She also knew she must part with her friends yet again. It was imperative they emigrate towards the warmth or perish.

It was not the first time she had begun to wonder why she had ever left her village to wander round a wasteland possibly for ever, but as soon as she broke open a pebble, her doubts dissipated as she saw a blue of such intensity that she felt more sure of herself. She called to Batwin and Freya.

"I have decided to make my way west to meet the ocean where the weather will be milder. But you two cannot survive in the winter without all the others. You would best fly north to meet them as soon as you can."

Freya shook her head.

"My precious Freya! It is my turn to be bossy. You both must leave before the strong winds arrive and blow you off course. I have warmth from my sac and this fruit so I will manage."

Pretzel tried to sound in charge but inside she felt bereft and kept feeling for her pebbles.

The birds twittered quietly in the trees before rejoining her.

"We have decided to fly North today."

"At last you are seeing reason, Batwin"

Again Pretzel was to experience those feather kisses, before watching the two fly off in their zigzag pattern before disappearing over the Goplin Thirkins. She hastily gathered up her belongings and turned away from the River Banzoor feeling a chill inside her even though the morning sun warmed her back.

*

As Marthamum prepared the evening meal she suddenly began to sing, "Pretzel is on her way home. I can feel it in my bones."

Drako looked at the shining face of his mother. It was the first time she had mentioned her name and wondered if she was losing her mind. What Gratacian has ever returned? Once left they joined the dead with no name. All Gratacians knew that, yet here was his mother with such hope in her eyes he could not bear it. He returned to his room to examine the three remaining stones in P. D's collar, glad now that he had kept them a secret for how could he explain their gradual disappearance? Poppo would have accused him of being foolhardy keeping them as his talisman in place of his sister. He knew there was another thing that Poppo and Marthamum never dared discuss. What if he wanted to follow his sister? He also knew now why no one ever mentioned his grandfather. He remembered the day he had found a goatskin wine bottle in the shed and his father hastily taking it from him with tears in his eyes and he never saw it again. Drako decided he must stay strong like Poppo and resist his flags when they appear.

He was woken in the night as his feet were freezing. He sat up to rub the circulation back into them before pulling on more leggings and another thick goat hair blanket, but lay there feeling like a lump of ice until the pallor of dawn.

*

When Pretzel reached the top of the first hillock she turned to look back at the river. She felt she was losing an old friend when it eventually disappeared from view. There were many icy streams to cross and she slipped often on the rocks cursing her shoes that were beginning to wear thin. The thorns from the ferns that edged the streams pierced Pretzel's clothing until she bled. She felt gladdened at first when she reached the top of a larger hill, only to find wave after wave of them continuing on as far as her eyes could see. She longed for the landscape to give a sign of change, some way of knowing that she would one day reach the sea, but she knew so little, what was she to look for. She recalled a painting on Reza's wall. There were words scrawled in the corner, 'The Billows'. She had seen Reza often looking at it with longing in her eyes at the green waves curling onto a sandy beach and it excited her to think that she may reach that ocean, if only she could arrive before her food supply ran out.

As the sun began to set, Pretzel dug out a hollow. The bruises from scrambling and slipping over the rocks were hurting. The night was long and again Pretzel became fearful. What would be the use of a pocket full of Vordak pebbles if she died of starvation or froze to death? But as soon as she broke one open her panic turned into a feeling of warmth as immediately before her was a blue painted ship steered by a big woman with red hair and a kind face. She knew then that all she had to do was to turn to them at any time.

Days passed monotonously except for the times she was able to explore her pebbles. The last of her pomoka were still green and were giving her a belly ache but there was no sign of any fruit bearing plants so had to make do. One morning she noticed deep clouds indicating a change in the weather, and sure enough the next day the mountains that still towered behind her were bright with snow. Despite her hunger she cried at their beauty and longed to share this moment with someone but the only companion was the wind, for there was no bird in the sky or beetle nestling in a rock to make friends with.

*

Harragar limped badly. Her knees were more swollen and her chilblains bothersome. She breathed more heavily when she slowly pulled herself up the ladder to collect her fruit. But despite her fading health, she was content. Now that the mudmen had left the area for good, her goats were multiplying. She smiled as she recalled her initial horror at seeing them arrive en masse thinking it was the last of her let alone her goats, then her delight when Buccasan revealed Pretzel's note. She had enjoyed neatening those brothers up before sending them on their way;

using some of her sheets to sew shirts for them all. She had cut their lank hair and ordered them to clean behind their ears. Eventually she waved them on, their stomachs filled with turnip soup, roast chicken, berry pie and goats cheese.

But after they had gone on their way and she was left alone again, she turned her mind to Pretzel, admonishing herself for not having gone part of the way, tired bones or not.

One night came when she dreamt of the Wattoo. It was no longer black but glowing red, and she now knew that this ominous void would never be as terrifying for anyone fool enough, gallant enough, or wise enough to explore, and she knew what ever Pretzel had achieved, her adventure into it was not wasted.

But when the first snows began to fall, Harragar started to fret for she knew Pretzel would not be passing back this way, at least not until the spring. She tossed and turned night after night, calling out, "Oh gal oh gal oh little gal," fearing the worst as tears ran down her wrinkled face until her pillow was soaked. She woke frequently, thumping her head and calling out into the blackness, but all that echoed back was the hush of snow fall, the occasional lament of an owl, and the groaning of the wind.

One morning, Harragar rose to milk the goats. It was still dark but the sky was clear with stars. She heard a fluttering in the trees, wondering where there would be birds this season, let alone before light. She heard them land on the roof and called out, hopefully.

"My golly snakes! Not you talking birds!"

As they landed in front of her, she recognized the unusual shaped beak of Batwin and cried with joy. She let Batwin and Freya into her room allowing them to dry their feathers by the stove, feast on berries and warm diluted goat's milk before listening to their story. Harragar laughed out loud, shaking her head when she heard about Pretzel slipping on the vines before heaving herself out, clapped her mouth shut as she listened about the leap into the Wattoo, slapped her thigh when Batwin described his return to retrieve another Tarzon topaz from the possum dog, hooted when Freya added that Pretzel had thrown it back into the Wattoo, and cried when she heard Pretzel was still out there, probably deep in the snow. She listened to their plan to retrieve the rest of the flock and in the meantime, she cooked up her berries, rolled out pastry and manufactured beak-sized tarts. She knitted hundreds of bird sized cloaks to protect each bird from the winter winds.

It was a thrilling moment for Harragar when she woke to be surrounded by the largest flock of birds she had seen in her life. She instructed them to take one small tartlet in each beak, and allow her to tie on each cloak to cover their wings, which took up most of the morning, before watching them line up behind Batwin. She stood on the hillock, the same one she had bad farewell to Pretzel all that time ago, waving her handkerchief until they were specks in the sky.

*

Pretzel woke with a knot in her belly. There were no more fruit and the last day she had broken off a piece of fern to munch.

"I'll pretend this is salad," she said hopefully.

The morning was overcast with just a shaft of sunlight peeping through cloud. She gazed with curiosity at a grey smudge approaching her which then formed into a brightly coloured funnel of flapping birds just like her first encounter by Lake Grataco except this time they were all colours of the rainbow. When she could make out their beaks she screamed with delight as they landed in front of her. Roland as usual circled above while in a few seconds Batwin and Freya were perching on her shoulder as if they had never left. Tachymus found a high rock shaking his head and looking as earnest and wise as ever as he surveyed her and Sorro turned somersaults with joy. To Pretzel's amazement, each bird deposited from their beak the smallest and most exquisitely made tartlet she had ever seen. She imagined Harragar sitting on her stool in the kitchen rolling out the pastry with her nobbly old hands and began to cry as Freya nestled into her pyjama pocket. She recognized the special tang of Harragar's jam and demolished a few of them as the wingflits pecked at the crumbs falling around her.

"What an unusual picnic this is!"

Pretzel was introduced to the newcomers for the winglets had been bountiful after the last nesting season.

Roland returned darting excitedly to and fro as Tachymus interpreted his message in the sky.

"We are going to the water. It is larger, much larger than Lake Grataco."

Pretzel knew they were inland birds, and had wondered how they would react when confronted with the huge waves. She wondered how she would react too.

"So. Here we are together again on another adventure, Batwin."

If a bird could sigh, Batwin did the nearest thing, shaking his head at this troublesome girl. But Pretzel could see he was just a little puffed up with pride. It was becoming obvious despite Batwin's complaints that he thrived on these challenges in his life. Why would a bird risk beak and feathers to drill out the precious topaz from the caves of Tarzon?

With renewed strength Pretzel tackled each hillock until after one steep climb Roland bobbed up and down with excitement.

"You have arrived," he twittered as he flew up again.

This hill was sandier than the ones before, and as soon as she reached the top she gasped at what did at first appear like Lake Grataco except it stretched to the horizon. She broke into a run, sliding down each sand dune, feeling as if she was approaching the Wattoo all over again, but this time instead of looking deep into the blackness, this was a massive expanse of blue which glinted and shifted before her eyes.

She stopped and sat in the sand, pouring it from one hand to the other, wishing Harragar could be with her now. She could have done with one of her mattresses to use as a toboggan. When Sorro joined Pretzel, he rolled in the sand with glee before shaking it off again all over her.

Pretzel reached the shore but stopped as a huge wave loomed up before her before crashing down with a roar. She turned and ran back to the nearest dune as the wingflits flew after her, squawking loudly until they saw it turn and recede back to where it came from, only to repeat its game over and over, regurgitating the patches of purple seaweed that had been lifted high in its belly. Pretzel felt as a small mammal might feel before being swallowed up by a snake. She ventured down to touch the water with her toes, before bending down to taste its saltiness on her lips. As she continued to watch the ocean, she began to understand why most Gratacians never return, for she was already becoming mesmerized, and the colours were more brilliant and varied than any of the blues and greens she had seen in Reza's dyes.

*

Poppo fished by the lake, hoping to catch the large bream he had seen lazily swimming by. Drako and P. D. joined him.

"Soon be spring, my boy."

Neither of them had wanted to discuss a spring without Pretzel.

'We have to make the most of it, heh Drako."

Drako looked away, trying to hide his tears but when he looked back, he noticed the lake was an unusual blue and as he watched it for a while he felt oddly comforted.

"Yes Poppo. We will make it festive as much as we can."

The wind suddenly picked up sending a fleck of foam from the lake onto Poppo's shirt.

"It's like an ocean today."

Drako nodded in agreement as the wavelets washed to and fro onto the shore. He felt a sense of wonder despite Poppo's sadness, for the lake appeared larger to him and the colour deeper. Not only that, when he had lifted his dog's fur to admire the topaz, they gave a distinct glow, as if they also were in preparation for something.

Poppo took him by the arm.

"Sit with me, son. You are all we have, you know."

CHAPTER 18   THE BETTIES

Pretzel covered the moist sand over her tired feet. She could have sat there for the rest of the day watching the changing blue of the sea, but was interrupted by Roland who had discovered an abundance of seed pods at the far end of the bay. He had indicated to Pretzel several times now that this was not their usual habitat and would need to adapt to their coastal surroundings and she was aware by the way he ruffled his neck feathers that he was not keen to stay here. He was already grumbling about the sand in his feathers and that fish was not to their taste. Pretzel pictured Harragar calling out, "What a lay-about lot of birds. Can't you catch a fish for gollysnakes? What are you good for then?"

She would have loved to share with Harragar the wonder of this wild ocean. When she opened a Vordak pebble it revealed an image of her riding the lumpy mattress over the waterfall, and expected she would float it on these huge waves if only she were here. Pretzel regretted not asking more questions of her wise old friend but no doubt she would have responded with, "Just one at a time, my girl, and you will find out." She realized now that Harragar had shown her that questions only appear when you are ready to ask them, and that the pebbles showed her images only when you are ready to see them.

She pulled herself up and limped along the beach to follow Roland. The sun was beginning to set and she stopped to watch until it formed a gold line on the horizon. By the time she caught up with the wingflits, they were already nesting in the tallest pines she had ever seen as she craned her neck to see where the commotion was coming from. When darkness fell she could see glimpses of light revealing a cluster of huts and stood feeling as if a tight shawl was wrapped around her. She felt suddenly fearful of intruding and wished she now had more of Harragar's feistiness, but already knew what her response would be, "Each to their own, my girl."

Pretzel decided to put off confronting the village folk until morning, and turned back towards the ocean. The sand felt cold on her bare feet as she walked along the shore. There was the dark shape of a jetty and at the base of it stood a shed. She peered through the window to see wet floor glistening in the moonlight and listened for any sign of life before heaving open the door. There was a dry patch in the corner above which hung a net smelling of rotting fish. As her eyes became more accustomed to the dark she made her way around the edge of the room and found a loaf of bread and an enamel pot with remnants of soup which she scraped off with her fingers. She could hear shouts and laughter in the distance and wished she had the courage to turn back towards them but felt too tired to deal with their questions. A young girl wandering along the beach followed by a flock of exotic birds isn't the norm anywhere let alone in the dead of night. She broke another pebble to give her comfort, seeing Harragar's face again and remembering her words, 'don't worry if your scared my girl.' Pretzel did feel afraid. She had been away from village people far too long. She would have to learn to explain herself again as the world was not made up totally of Harragars and wingflits. She tried to sleep but the coldness of the ground seeped through her cocoon sac and when the moon set she lay shivering in the darkness.

At first light Freya flew in twittering with excitement. Sorro dipped his wings in a puddle of oily water, which stuck to his feathers and which he endeavoured to remove by flapping his wings in the sand. Pretzel felt in better humour as she watched his antics, but when she heard the sounds of the villagers, she had to take a deep breath before approaching them. A group of women who were repairing massive nets hanging from the trees looked up with surprise.

"Hey, young lady!"

"Hello, I am...."

"How did you arrive these parts? There wasn't a boat arrive, was there?""

"I walked here."

They stopped their work in amazement as curious women and children surrounded Pretzel. She noted that the older women were wearing red checked aprons and clucking together like hens, the young girls in simple dresses of light pastels pranced around on slender limbs like wading birds, while the infants carried on their hips were clothed in brilliantly coloured jumpsuits appearing to her like parrots. She then realized she had been away from civilization far too long, for she was now seeing her fellow human beings as a different breed of bird.

"Walked from where?" The women chorused, staring at Pretzel in amazement.

"I was walking in the Goplin Thirkins with my backpack and took longer than I planned. Fortunately I had a friend who gave me plenty of food in case of such a situation like this happening and she cooked for me plenty of tarts so I wouldn't go hungry. Then the snows arrived earlier than expected so I thought if I went due west I would reach the ocean and well.... that's it really."

The old ladies shook their heads as the young girls giggled at her clothes. Reza's pyjamas did look a bit out of place here.

"Well, young woman, you must eat with us."

One of the girls reached out to touch Pretzel's hair.

"Where's your manners, little Betty? Run and bring a bowl of mussel chowder. What's your name?"

"I am….known as Pretzel."

"We are Betty."

"Which one is Betty?"

"We all are. It is good luck to be called Betty so we all are named Betty."

"Oh… Then how do you know when to answer?"

"We all answer. No squabbles then."

"Right, Betty."

It appeared to be the right thing to say as the women laughed and one slapped Pretzel on the back, making her spill the thick soup down her front which caused more whooping and cheers until it seemed to her that Harragar was a picture of Gratacian conformity compared to this group, but she was in no position to complain.

A young girl handed her a loaf of bread.

"Break it off, Betty."

"Thank you, but my name is Pretzel…. or... Betty, I suppose."

The women clapped their hands and it was obvious to Pretzel she had made the appropriate reply.

A child suddenly called out with delight as she pointed to the trees. The wingflits had been keeping a safe distance, but it was no longer possible to conceal the fact they were strangers to this part of the country. Pretzel thought quickly.

"They have been following me. I gave them the crumbs from my tarts. They became quite tame and now …you will see they are my friends for they haven't yet flown away."

The Betties accepted this explanation and began to break up the loaf, throwing the crumbs beneath the trees. Roland first flew down followed by dozens of winglets that pecked away in the grass to the delight of the children who ran amongst them making them fly to see the green under their wings.

Pretzel wondered about the men folk. She thought of the mudmen, and wondered if some terrible accident had befallen their men in a similar way, but it came obvious when a Betty pointed out to sea.

"The men are away with the boats. The young boys go out with them too."

A large woman named Big Betty took Pretzel by the arm and led her through the village. The huts looked neat and cosy. Most of them had an annexe attached to allow for the summer breezes, but this time of year the winds were still cold so they were used for storage of tackle. There were rows of leather coats and boots, all heavily oiled, with that now familiar smell of fish emanating from them. Big Betty showed her the rough cloth the women dyed, quite different from Reza's silks, the fishing lines and nets they prepared, and the pots they wove to catch the giant lobster deep beneath the ocean. Numerous tawny hens clucked around them which Big Betty frequently shooed away. The hens mostly ignored her and kept getting under her feet. A rooster crowed followed by the sound of a baby gurgling in delight. It appeared to Pretzel that it was a cheerful village which was much smaller but not unlike Grataco in its conviviality.

Pretzel stopped in front of one of the houses. This one was painted a bright lime green and appeared larger and more comfortable. A woman who was swathed in a deep purple shawl stood at her door. Big Betty watched bemused as Pretzel leant forward to take a closer look at the stone on the window sill, glowing red in the morning light.

"That is called a Tarzon topaz. A man once visited here on the supply ship and enquired after a boat of his own. Our men refused until he showed Lucky Betty's man what he had as currency. Now that the upkeep of our boats cost so much more, a new one would be worth at least three of those if we could get our hands on any more of them. We are all very content with our lot but we could do with more money to repair our boats. And we need more nets but we make do. But we do worry about our men out there and the safety of our aging vessels."

"Its time to collect the firewood!" a woman with a thick plait of red hair sung out.

"Right you are, Betty love."

Pretzel helped collect the kindling from under the trees and as soon as she was out of sight, whispered a greeting to Freya.

"I am safe here. Freya, don't fret."

Freya landed on Pretzel's shoulder.

"Won't fret won't fret."

Pretzel felt a shiver of pleasure from the downy feathers on her cheek before she returned to the safety of the pines.

Pretzel deposited the branches onto a pile as Big Betty explained.

"The men are on their way home. We all feel it in our bones that it will be tonight, so we are preparing the bonfire and will light it as soon as it is dark. They will find us more easily and then you'll see how we all celebrate! We Betties sure know how to kick up our heels!"

Pretzel followed the women down to the beach. Most of them had golden plaits down their back that swung as they walked. They stacked the branches to an enormous height. Now that the children had lost their initial shyness, they chattered around her, asking endless questions with a lilting accent that was at times difficult to understand. It reminded her of the ebb and flow of the sea. She assumed by their questions that they had never known snow, mountains or desert, let alone Catoa, or the strange city of the Saradens which seemed a lifetime away. Pretzel felt a surge of envy for their simple life. In one way it was similar to her home and again those feelings of guilt troubled her. She knew there would be many of her stories the Betties may never understand and she felt pierced by their curious glances. She sensed there was no way she could explain why she had walked out on her own village with the love and comforts it offered. How could she describe the Wattoo to these folk? They would think her crazy. She wouldn't dare begin. She began to imagine now that if she would be the first ever to return to Grataco and show them her wondrous find, how they would respond. No doubt they would sit wide eyed and listen to her tales late into the night over and over.

"Yes. I must bring them home," she said to herself, feeling their comfortable warmth in her pocket, "and perhaps I will be famous."

The women lit the fire as soon as the sun began to set and stood around staring out to sea.

"We are listening for the sound of the horn. Every few moments we must stay quiet."

The children all knew that when Big Betty raised her hand they must stop their chattering and babbling. Just as the sun became a rim of red on the horizon, Big Betty called out, "They're coming!"

The women stood on the beach in silence. Pretzel noticed tears rolling down the face of Big Betty as she fell on her knees and began to pray. Pretzel thought of the occasional tragic deaths from mountain avalanches or rock falls, but had taken for granted the rare and sumptuous fish feasts which at times appeared in Grataco. Most Gratacian families had a Poppo like her own, but here she was struck by the danger in what the men did for a living.

The women returned to stoke up the fire, explaining it would take a while for the fishermen to moor the boats and off load their haul. They joyfully threw on more logs until shouts were heard above the wash of the sea.

Big Betty placed the lamb on the spit. An assortment of salads, fig cakes, mountains of turkey legs, and potatoes were carried out by the children to the long wooden table that stood on the sand.

"They will want something other than fish," Big Betty explained. "And my Vagya loves his lamb."

No one ate until the boats were anchored and the fishermen were beached, washed, kissed and seated. Then as one, each man, woman, and child hoed in heartily. Pretzel remained unnoticed, also helping herself to large portions, and it wasn't until after all the loud burps followed that one of the men put down his knife and stared at Pretzel.

"Eh! Big Betty! By' ere who come she?"

"She's a walker."

The fisherman put his face so close to Pretzel that she could feel the whiskers tickle her cheek. Despite all the scrubbing beforehand, he smelt of fish and seaweed.

"You from the North I see that. The nose and the black hair…ya a beauty girlie."

"Domto! Caution now! She's not a sheep in the yard to be checked out like that."

But Pretzel's mind was already busy with other things. As much as she was welcome here, and perhaps now with this man called Domto, too welcome, she was keen to reach home as fast as it was possible. Perhaps she would arrive before the next Springfest. For the moment though, she would need to behave like a welcome guest. She was relieved when Domto suddenly become more interested in the wine than herself, so none of them noticed her quietly extracting herself from the group to check on the wingflits.

Next morning Domto examined the nets, marking out the holes with twine for the women to repair. He stopped when Pretzel passed him.

"Ah! What a sight for me eyes, my girl!"

Pretzel ignored the remark but chose to question him all the same.

"Excuse me, er... Domto. Can you advise me the best way to travel north from here? I need to return to Grataco, my village, as soon as possible."

He spat out a leaf.

"There are no more villages along the coast for a long way. No fresh water. You're better off staying with us, young lady."

"Would I be able to go by boat?"

"No chance. They are back here now till mid spring."

He took a step closer to Pretzel.

"Why are you in such a rush now?"

She took a step back.

"Because I must continue on my way home as soon as possible."

"No chance, girl."

"Can I not hire a fishing boat to take me?"

Domto slapped his plump thigh and snorted particles of leaf over Pretzel.

"We catch fish. We don't take girls for day trips. Well, perhaps pretty ones like you.... perhaps."

Pretzel tried to ignore Domto's remark and wished Big Betty was with her now. She felt more and more discomforted by his leering stare which made her more determined to find a way out of this village.

"I hear someone bought one of your boats."

"You buy a boat. What with?"

Domto was enjoying himself watching her discomfort.

"I must go back to help Big Betty."

Pretzel hurried away feeling the harshness of Domto's laughter penetrate her backbone. She found Big Betty shaking out her mats.

"Betty. Could I stay and earn my keep until I can afford to buy a boat to take me home?"

Big Betty held Pretzel by the shoulders and looked into her face.

"It's a long wait girlie. You look pale. ... Is it that Domto bothering you? He hasn't a wife you see. That's his trouble. But Big Betty will look after you. Oh my dear, you are crying."

She hugged Pretzel who almost disappeared inside her wide frame.

"You can live with me, Vagya and the littlies. We can work the nets together. You're safe with me, dearie."

The day dragged on for Pretzel and as soon as night fell, she ventured out to the trees.

"Batwin, I have to talk to you," she whispered.

Batwin followed Pretzel along the beach until she was well out of earshot.

"I have an idea how we can all get away."

For a while they talked together as Batwin huffed and flapped his wings, soon joined by Freya and Tachymus. The three birds flew back to the trees to twitter late into the night as Pretzel crept back to her bed beside Big Betty.

Next morning, Pretzel woke early and walked along the beach as the wingflits blithely flew around her, much to the amusement of the men working on the jetty. She continued on until safely out of their hearing range.

"What have you all decided, Tachymus? "

Tachymus turned and faced the wingflits, "We are land birds, not seabirds. The salt sticks to our feathers, and the fish smells get up our beaks. If the girl has a plan, hear her out."

"Out, out, out," twittered the winglets.

"I must say that Batwin has helped me enough already I know, and I am exceedingly grateful."

Sorro flew down and balanced on one wing before falling into the sand, as Roland circled above before landing amongst them.

"There are good winds from the South. If you have decided, the best time to leave is now."

Batwin chose two sturdy winglets that flapped around him excitedly.

The men stopped their fish processing and looked up in surprise, as three birds flew in a zigzag pattern before flying northward.

*

Drako was woken by the full moon shining in though the window. He sat up and gazed in awe at the snow glistening in the valley. He was glad however, that the days were beginning to lengthen, and always looked forward to the melt causing numerous waterfalls which fed into the lake turning it a milky blue. He also loved the clear skies that preceded spring. He was continuing to look out at the tree shadows as stark as in daylight when three birds landed on the window sill. One of then had an odd shaped beak.

"Must have been attacked by something," he surmised.

It flew directly to P.D.'s collar and deftly picked out the three remaining stones. The smaller birds then followed suit, each gathering a topaz in its beak before appearing again at the windowsill. There was a final flash of red in the moonlight before they disappeared into the night. Drako stroked his dog's neck and as he looked at the spaces in the collar, and couldn't help feeling a mixture of loss and wonder.

CHAPTER 19   DOMTO

Pretzel turned back along the shore and hurried past the fishermen's curious stares. She was aware now she must be patient, stay close to Big Betty and hope that the wingflits will cope with yet another long wait. She had seen Sorro amusing them all with his daily sand baths in attempt to placate them all, as there were frequent loud grumblings at the wind that continually blew sand into their beaks. That night she crept past the sounds of heavy snoring and called to Freya who flew down immediately. Pretzel could feel her trembling.

"Try not to worry, Freya. Remember the winds are against them on their return and the topaz will slow them down so it will be many a long night before we will see them again. But we will. You know our Batwin. He is strong and brave. "

Suddenly Freya began to tremble more violently and flew off frantically back to the trees.

"What is the matter, Freya? Speak to me."

Pretzel heard the sound of crackling of leaves behind her as a hand clapped her mouth shut before she could scream. The familiar fish smell of Domto was overpowering, as the wingflits, now visible in the grey light, watched helplessly from above.

"So, not only do you have them birds feeding outa your hand, you have taught them to speak!"

Pretzel cursed herself for letting her guard down so badly.

"Yes, Domto," as he released his hand from her mouth, "They have been with me for a long time and they gradually picked up my sounds."

"No, my little lady! Domto isn't as stupid as he looks. I heard them speak sentences. You can't tell me they are ornery birds. We can make lots of money from these if we put them in a circus."

"No. They will never be used in a circus. They are wild."

"Wild birds don't talk proper like this."

"They have become tame and mimic me, that's all."

"But they will perform for us, Little Betty! When you become my wife we will leave this place full of demanding and bossy women and make our fortune with these here talkin' birds."

Pretzel's heart thumped loudly in her ears.

"No. No. They will fly off for ever if you suggest such a thing."

"You mean to say they understand you as well?"

Pretzel felt she was more and more in hot water.

"No. They just mimic me…"

"Don't give me that…They are smarter than that… What a find!"

Domto let Pretzel go from his grip.

"All I need to do is to tell the others what I have seen. Then they will trap them and sell them in exchange for boats. They all need the money too badly to treat them just as pets, young lady."

Pretzel had to think how to get out of this terrible predicament for she knew the wingflits would never leave her and would risk being caught to stay with her. She felt sick at the thought of Freya being imprisoned yet again and knew she was perched above listening, still and silent in the tree above.

"Domto! These birds will not talk to anybody else but me."

"Then you talk, they talk, and I collect the money."

Domto slapped his thigh as Pretzel shivered.

"No more fishing here for I'm out of this godforsaken place as soon as I can. No more of these pushy Betties who get up my snoz. Just you and me, hey, Beauty?"

Pretzel wanted to be sick again but had to think fast. The man was determined but what gratified her was that he seemed also gullible.

"Domto! Please don't tell the others about the talking birds and I will think of something...how you can get away."

"Only if you promise."

"Promise what?"

"Be my wife and run away from here."

"How will that be possible?"

"We steal a boat."

"We can't. They need every one. These are your people, Domto!"

"My people, Fat Galopa fish! I will tell them I am taking take you for a little ride around the bay. They will think we are coming back but instead we turn north."

Pretzel was disgusted at his plan of betrayal and the thought of spending even a minute on any boat with him was out of the question. She had no choice, however, but to go along with him for the moment until she could think of something better.

"I have a different idea on how we can leave here for good but I cannot tell you yet."

"You're hedging my girl."

"If I go along with your plan the birds will fly off. They will be nesting soon and then will not leave their little ones. I am earning my keep to buy a boat and then we can leave here together. It will be wise in the meantime not to be seen with me so the Betties won't gossip, and stay away from these trees, for the birds might become more anxious and fly away in any case."

To her relief she sounded convincing. After he was gone, Pretzel whispered, "Trust me, precious wingflits. We will all have to be more careful now. Just behave like ordinary birds as much as you can."

Pretzel joined Big Betty who was wringing out the clothes.

"You were talking a long time with Domto. He is a lonely one, but harmless. He needs a wife to change his ways and smarten him up a bit and all."

"I am not a thing, Big Betty! I am not ready to be anyone's wife, or handmaiden or anything."

Big Betty put the clothes down.

"But is that not what all young women dream of?"

"Not for me and surely not with... that Domto."

"But he is a good man, and he likes you, I see."

"I am not ready. And in any case, I am homesick."

Betty enclosed Pretzel in her arms.

"Wait!"

She walked over to Domto who was making himself busy rolling up the nets but watching the women out of the corner of his eye.

"Listen! Don't get any designs on the new girl. She is not grown up enough, not like our village girls, so she would not be a suitable wife for you anyway. Leave her alone or I'll give you a hiding!"

"Right, right."

He gave Pretzel a wink before gathering up the nets and carrying them away to the shed.

"He's a bit rough around the edges, but is a kind man, really."

Pretzel felt it prudent just to nod.

"Growing up is hard, eh? Come on. We have more sheets to hang out."

As the weeks went on, there was plenty to keep Pretzel oc-
cupied. She learnt quickly the knots required to repair the nets.
She already knew how to make a delicious goat's cheese recipe
which she taught the women. As she had become strong from
her mountain climbing, she managed to carry heavy bundles of
wood, feeling satisfied she was earning her keep. The hardest part
was having to reassure the wingflits that she was not about to betray them, for to them she appeared as if she was going along with
Domto's plan. She guessed it must be difficult for a wingflit that
lived a life of simplicity to learn that humans could be so devious.

The winglets hatched when they days became warmer. At
last a morning came when Pretzel was taking the aprons off the
line. She looked up to see three specks in the sky coming towards
her and as soon as she was alone she waved. Batwin and his two
winglets quickly swooped down and dropped their stones into
the basket before disappearing into the trees. She pocketed them
just as Big Betty carried out another load.

"Why, Little Betty! You have more colour in your cheeks.
This weather is doing you good."

That same evening, when the village folk were seated
around the table, Pretzel finished serving the meal but remained
standing. She looked over at Domto.

"I have something to tell you all."

The group stopped their usual banter to listen.

"Now that Spring in on its way I plan to leave for my village, Grataco. I wish to buy a boat together with the loan of a
skipper."

Big Betty began to wail. Domto sat open mouthed while
one of the other men laughed.

"And what makes you think you can buy one of our boats?"

"All of you will be able to buy faster boats and what is
more, the one I purchase from you will be returned."

"She is talking in riddles."

They watched with bemusement as Pretzel felt inside her pockets, but when she deposited each topaz on the table, they gaped in amazement. Big Betty stopped wailing and clapped her hand over her mouth while Domto found his voice.

"Where you got them, girl?" he croaked.

"From near my village. I have carried them as a talisman and have not said anything as they are for good luck and did not want to part with them. I saw that one of you has one in the window over there which served you well, but insufficient now due to the higher costs of fishing boats. I would need many moons to earn enough for a boat so…these will be yours, if you will kindly allow me to purchase a boat and the loan of a skipper and then you will have your boat back. I have no need of it in Grataco, for we live far from the sea."

The group passed the stones around, holding them towards the fire light to see them glow and nodded agreement, thrilled that the deal was so in their favour.

Domto raised his hand, but Big Betty interrupted him.

"I will take her. You, Domto are needed here. I can skipper it as well as anyone. My father taught me well, not like you younger Betties. We did all the work of the men in our day."

"It is settled then."

One by one The Betties and their men shook Pretzel's hand until it was Domto's turn.

"Trust me. Do nothing for the moment. Meet me under the tree after dark," she whispered.

Her heart was beating fast. Never before had she double crossed anyone in her life. Her head was aching from the tension as she needed to speak to the wingflits before Domto arrived.

"We are leaving in just a few days as soon as the boat is prepared. You needn't fly out to sea, but can follow us along the coast."

"Grataco, Grataco." The winglets chirped, becoming quiet at the sound of Domto's steps.

"What is this all about? Remember my warning. It still stands. These people here will know about them talking birds if you dare double cross me."

"Domto! My plan is this. When you come down to farewell us, I will think of something to make Big Betty return to her hut, something important she may have forgotten, and then you take the helm."

Pretzel was relieved that Domto was so struck by her innocent expression that he accepted her plan readily. She became aware of Big Betty, her hands on her hips, looking over at them.

"Domto! You must leave me now, or she will suspect something is afoot."

As soon as he was out of earshot, Pretzel called up to Tachymus.

"I am taking a walk along the beach."

He knew that signal well by now as he waited until she was well around the point before joining her. Pretzel explained her plan to him, knowing the group will go along with it under his guidance. When she returned to meet Big Betty, they discussed late into the night what provisions they would need: loaves of bread, figs, beans and tomatoes for their journey to supplement the fish they would catch.

Big Betty put her arms around Pretzel.

"The winds are in the right direction, and will blow us all the way to Port Prohsorm."

The night before they were to depart Pretzel felt tinges of fear, hoping her plan would not backfire. She then remembered her pebbles which she had forgotten in her excitement. She was shown the bluest of ocean and thick purple clouds from which shone rays of gold.

*

The days were now warm enough for the goats to be released from their enclosures to run free up the mountain slopes. It was always a pleasure for Marthamum and Poppo to see them bounding up each hillock, their tails vibrating. Tufts of new bright green grass were lit up by the morning sun.

*

Drako brushed P.D. until he was glossy. Some days he felt heavy hearted now all his stones were gone and regretted not hiding them in a better place, but something told him other wise. Perhaps the arrival of those strange birds was an omen that his sister was trying to send a message. He couldn't hope she would return as he knew that was out of the question. Despite that, one thing worried him enormously. He knew only too well the Gratacian rule regarding possum dogs that they belonged to every one. He felt guilty for having mixed feelings about wanting his sister to return at all, as that would mean having to relinquish his beloved animal back to the Village Square.

CHAPTER 20   ABOARD THE BETTINA

Next morning, Big Betty gathered up reels of fishing lines together with an assortment of hooks that Pretzel had never seen before. The small ones she recognized for catching Lake Grataco bream, but she wondered at the size of sea creature that would be lured to a hook the size of her fist. Pretzel recalled how the Hetzenbabel used its large hook like appendage to snare the wingflits, and wondered what lay below in that vast ocean. She glanced at Big Betty who was humming away to herself quite unperturbed, and felt less anxious.

There was a festive air in the village, mixed with loud sniffles as the Betties carried the cargo down to the jaunty green boat tied to the jetty. The name 'Bettina' was painted on the side. Big Betty explained that Betty was such a lucky name in this village that no one dared to call their boat otherwise. The newer boats had the sea's gifts added to their name. Hence 'Bettfish', 'Bettgull', 'Bettcrab', and 'Bettsquid 'were bobbing up and down on their anchors.

"You be coming back now, Little Betty," a woman called, kissing Pretzel again and again. Each Betty followed, giving her a bag of their precious figs.

"Of course, one day I will return to see you all."

"Time to leave where there is still plenty of day. We must be well past the reef before the tide changes," Big Betty called, stepping with ease onto the Bettina, despite her large frame, but Pretzel balked at stepping off the jetty onto the boat which seemed to her to be pulling at the ropes to escape.

"Not traveled by sea, Little Betty?"

Pretzel pointed to the horizon. "Never. I have not been by any ocean until I came to see the Billows, and now I am to go way out there. I'm a bit nervous, Big Betty."

She saw Domto arriving with his swag and looked anxiously at the trees as he followed her onto the boat.

"What are you wanting, Domto!" Big Betty called out as she proceeded to untie the rope.

"I have a gift for Little Betty,"

But it was not long before Domto realized he had been hoodwinked, for Pretzel was making no attempt to distract or remove Big Betty from the boat. He stepped toward Big Betty, and was about to grab her plump arm when he found himself surrounded by squawking birds that pecked at him furiously, not letting up until he was off the gangplank. He kicked and slapped at the wingflits that continued to circle around him until the Bettina was well out of reach.

Pretzel blew kisses into the wind, "Thank you, my beloved wingflits."

"I've never seen the likes of that, my girl. Those birds sure know how to protect you."

Pretzel felt the water beneath her. It was like being on the back of a heaving monster.

It was not long before the trees became dots and the boat rocked more violently, but as soon as Big Betty had steered the Bettina beyond the reef, the sea became calm again and she was able to talk to Pretzel.

"My! That Domto was a keen one. Those bird friends of yours sure were determined to keep him off the Bettina!"

At last Pretzel was able to relate the circumstances she found herself in, with Domto planning to betray the village. Big Betty was tight lipped as she steered the boat northward.

"There will be no place for him at our village unless he sees the error of his ways. .... and where will they be now? The birds I mean?"

"Following us along the coast."

Pretzel crouched on the floor, hanging tightly on to a rope. She had tried to stand, but it was like being in a slippery dip.

"If Harragar was here she would be whooping." Pretzel thought, but she was feeling sick.

"You are the colour of the boat, Little Betty. Chew on this."

Big Betty handed her what appeared to be an old strip of leather, which she bit into gingerly until the nausea dissipated.

"An old secret. The men take it with them. Dry meat soaked in malakoberry juice."

Pretzel slowly began to enjoy the colour of the inky blue sea with its tail of white foam, while the throb of the engine began to soothe her nerves.

"At night we follow the northern star," Big Betty explained. "You can take the till if I sleep and just hold it still. There are no rocks until just before we arrive at Port Prohsorm."

But at this stage Pretzel was happy to wander in a crab like way around the deck and exploring the tiny little kitchen below.

"Galley fits only one person. You can have a go at dinner Little Betty, and tomorrow I will give you a fishing line. You have fished?"

"With my Poppo on the lake. Just small bream only."

Big Betty began to sing in a deep guttural voice in a language Pretzel had never heard before.

It was not until late afternoon, when Big Betty turned around and saw what appeared to be a black funnel following the boat. She screamed as the funnel became closer, becoming a swish of wings. To Pretzel's amusement, Big Betty let go of the wheel causing the boat to turn in circles, gasping as hundreds of birds descended onto the boat. Their yellow beaks flashed in the afternoon sun as they perched along the deck. The wingflits turned their heads from side to side to survey Big Betty.

"Those birds won't let you alone now. I've never seen the likes of such a thing!"

Pretzel was in her element and so relieved to be again with her beloved wingflits, that she forgot Big Betty who was busy realigning the boat.

"Freya, Batwin, Tachymus, Roland and my dear little Sorro," she called delightedly, "How I have missed you already."

Big Betty turned from the wheel and frowned at Pretzel. "Those malokaberries are sending you a bit off your rocker, little Betty."

Pretzel no longer cared what Big Betty thought of her as she greeted her friends. Big Betty shook her head at Pretzel and sighed.

"Here take the wheel and I will make you a strong fig drink. That will set you right."

"Careful not to tread on the winglets," called Pretzel as Big Betty stomped past the flapping of wings to get to the galley.

"Winglets!" Big Betty muttered. "The sooner I off load this poor girl and her feathered followers the better. Too much sun and sizzled brains, that's what!"

"We are not sea birds," Roland twittered anxiously.

"Yes I realize that you are not meant to be off land but here you are, becoming seabirds. If you all stay with the boat and pretend it is a small island, it will be easier for you all." Freya perched on Pretzel's shoulder and for yet another time Pretzel could feel her trembling.

"Wingflits! I hope this will be your last adventure. Then you can go home, wherever that is. . Or… I hope it will be wherever my home is." stammered Pretzel.

Freya rested her beak on Pretzel's ear. "Never leave, never leave."

As the sun was setting in a crimson ball, Pretzel threw crumbs to the wingflits, hoping it would not be long before they reached land. Once Big Betty had returned and had got over her initial shock, she laughed.

"Well, we have had stowaways before but never the likes of these! Here take the wheel while I watch you handle the boat."

Pretzel felt happier now that the wingflits were not too unwelcome. The sea became pitch black, the stars above intense and in time each bird was asleep, beaks now tucked well in under their wings. Pretzel stared at the occasional white of a wave breaking and tried to imagine what lived below. Big Betty took the wheel from Pretzel, whose turn was to lie on the bunk, listening to the creaking and lapping below.

She broke open a Wattoo pebble and immediately saw faces of lost fishermen, skeletons beneath the sea, a huge tentacled creature with one sad eye, cavorting sea horses, and platoons of yellow striped fish. She then saw Harragar tossing and turning as if on a ship sailing her mattress into the deep inky blue.

Freya flew down to be with Pretzel, twittering softly until she slept. Freya pecked at one of the pebbles in Pretzels' palm but left it, as it was inedible.

Next morning, Pretzel clambered up to find that Big Betty was pouring tea into ramekins and singing with gusto, "Figs for breakfast. Figs figs. Figs is good for you and me."

She chortled. "Hope you weren't hoping for a change. Here birdies!"

She broke up some pieces as the wingflits swooped down.

"You didn't wake me, Big Betty."

"Time to get your sea legs. This morning, you can steer while I take a nap, and then we do some fishing, Hey birdies! Cant you catch fish!"

"They eat seeds and insects. They are not sea birds."

Big Betty shook her head before squeezing her frame below. Pretzel felt more confident being in charge of the wheel, with Freya close to her ear.

When Big Betty climbed up again, it was well past noon.

"Now we throw these lines over and see what the sea will give us today!"

It seemed only minutes before Pretzel felt a massive jerk.

"Don't let it go. Haul it in girl."

Big Betty set the Bettina on course and went to help her.

"Thought as much! Galopa fish are common these parts. Not bad for a feed."

A massive blue finned fish appeared at the surface, and the two women pulled it in.

"Here. I will put it out of its misery. Can't bear to see these things die suffocating."

Big Betty smashed its head with a hammer and soon the fish lay still as the wingflits watched in silence.

"Like a funeral!" she laughed.

Days went by as each changed shift. One night, Pretzel fell asleep at the wheel, but as soon as the boat was off course, Big Betty was up beside her.

"You are lucky your old Betty has second sight. My body knows if have switched direction"

"It won't happen again. I am so ashamed."

'It was a tall order, little Betty. All that responsibility when you have never been near the ocean. Here get some sleep, and next time, wake me if you are tired. Anyways, can't those friends help you?"

"They are not sea going birds, but I will ask them to help me stay awake on the night watch."

There was no further mishap and till one morning, Big Betty woke Pretzel.

"All hands on deck! This is the rough part of our passage. It is the furthest from the coast where there is no protection. We toss a bit so drink up fast or you'll be spraying those birds with tea."

Up till now Pretzel had likened the ocean to a winter storm on Lake Grataco, but as the waves began to rear up higher than the boat, Pretzel became alarmed that they would eventually capsize, like the canoes on Lake Grataco but this time, there would be no shore to swim to. She wondered what they do if they capsized. Big Betty seemed to read Pretzel's mind.

"These boats don't roll over. They ride the waves, you'll see."

The wingflits were not so convinced. Each time the boat dipped in a furrow they flew above in frenzy then resettled as the boat crested, only to repeat the same over and over. Pretzel was so amused at their antics that she forgot her own fears. By mid afternoon the sea flattened more as Big Betty turned the boat eastwards.

"Now we surf to Prohsorm, for the wind is behind us. Once past the Rock, it is just like walking. The rock is called Rock Triskh, after the first ship that collided with it. I will take the till from now on, as there is a hidden reef around it. Our fisherman have made up a ditty, 'We don't risk with Triskh' as many a poor coot has broken up his boat on it. Just not keeping a watch out, simple as that."

The wingflits squawked excitedly. Sorro swooped this way and that, followed by his usual attempts to balance on one wing.

"That bird is a bit of a clown," remarked Big Betty.

"Yes. It seems that way." Pretzel replied carefully. She would have liked to tell Big Betty more about Sorro's antics in the forest, but it would have meant having to explain too much.

"Aha. There she is, the risky Rock Triskh."

Big Betty slowed the engine down to a low throb, passing the rock with ease. Pretzel leaned over the edge to survey the reef with the foam of water swirling around it. It gave a sucking sound that made her shudder.

Now that they were out of danger, Big Betty concentrated on the line of land. By late afternoon the sun shone on what appeared to be white teeth, later becoming tall silos as they became closer. As the sun began to set, twinkling lights appeared. The water was a pale shimmer as they inched towards the long jetty. Pretzel was so overcome with excitement that she did not see the large tears rolling down Big Betty's cheeks.

*

Marthamum passed a bowl of soup to Drew. She had such a feeling of joy at the thought of warm air, street theatres, and spring in Grataco. She felt in her bones that Pretzel was on her way home, hoping it was not her imagination getting the better of her. She did not see the large tear running down Drew's cheeks as he stroked his possum dog.

CHAPTER 21   PORT PROHSORM

Big Betty lassoed the post, calling out instructions to Pretzel who stepped off on to the pier unsteadily, feeling as if the water was still continuing to heave under her.

"The ocean is reminding you of its rhythm Little Betty. You'll soon feel your balance return."

Pretzel hung on to a post and looked up at the sky. As soon as they had reached the Port the wingflits had flown off to shore, but only two gulls hovered above.

"They will be having a fine feast of grain from the silos, poor things... I will miss those little bird friends of yours, but as for you my girl, you are a daughter to me now."

Two boys fishing from the pier watched with curiosity as the two linked arms. One of them called out, '"Hey, Betty! Your boat could do with a coat of paint."

"None of your lip, laddie! She's going to have one as soon as I get her home again. But what about you both! Just take a look at your overcoats. If you were ships you'd sink to the bottom quick smart!"

"Any figs by any chance?"

"Well, if you both help keep an eye on the Bettina you can have some."

"Who's your little mate, Betty?"

"An intrepid walker who landed at our village. She is on her way home. Been a way too long, I think, hey little Betty?"

"Not another Betty!"

"None of your teasing! You know about our funny ways… Well, we must be up the hill before it gets pitch dark. Say hello to your mamas for I wont be seeing them this time as I'm off in the morning with the tide. I'm hoping I can persuade Marika on the hill to come back for company."

"You'll have to persuade her. She hardly ever comes down to the shops, let alone to the ocean."

"I don't blame her with cheeky lads like you lolling about!"

They left the boys and continued towards the silos that had stood out so clearly from the ocean, but there was no sign of the wingflits.

"They'll be gorging themselves. Talking of a good feast, my old friend Marika will put us up but we have some climbing to do. See that orange light on the top of the hill. That's what we are aiming for."

They turned along a street which wound round past wooden cottages, each with lattice protecting the front porches.

"They sleep out there in summer. It gets so hot up here. I'm glad we live on top of the ocean, well, almost. But Marika has the right idea living up there to get the breezes. Trouble is, the winter storms buffet her about something terrible. Poor Marika. She believes in no manner of odd ghosts and whatever and talks to every animal she sees. In fact she's a bit like you come to think of it."

They passed a row of fish shops closing for the night. Pretzel recognised the sad eyes of the Galopa fish in the window. The vendor limped out to greet Big Betty and stared at Pretzel as he smoothed his black strands of hair over his scalp.

"Got this leg caught between the jetty and my boat so I'm off fishing for a season. Who's your mate?"

"A traveller. She calls herself Pretzel."

"And you call her….now let me guess…"

"None of your mocking kind sir... This is Bikorn but we call him Bik."

"Hello, Bik."

"Where did you get those pyjamas?"

Pretzel looked down and blushed.

"It was cold on the boat."

Big Betty farewelled Bik and they continued on. Pretzel turned and saw him still standing outside his door watching her.

"This port is not safe at night. And your outfit sure attracts their attention. Marika will find something for you to wear so you won't stand out like God's gift to all parrots."

As they began to climb Pretzel turned frequently to look at the view below. The lights twinkled around the harbour now black and glistening. Far out to sea a light flashed which she assumed came from Rock Trishk. A smell of fish from the processing factory followed them until they were higher. A terrier yapped at a gate and through the window she could see a family grouped around the table. The smell of barbecued meat reminded her of what she had craved when on the Bettina for she had become tired of their total diet of fish.

The path narrowed and became steeper. Pretzel enjoyed exercising her legs again while Big Betty puffed alongside her. At last they reached Marika's gate which shuddered on its hinge as they opened it.

"This also could do with a coat of paint," mumbled Betty as she dragged it shut. When they entered the porch, also enclosed by lattice, an aroma of onions greeted them.

"She's seen the boat and got wind up we're coming. Oh, Hi luvvy!"

There were whoops from both the women as they embraced each other.

"It has been too long my dear and..."

"This young lady arrived on foot, gave us all a surprise, and she is keen to get home so came with me on the Bettina. She paid her way, but that is another story. More of that later."

Marika was tall and thin, not unlike Harragar in build. Her startling green eyes creased with smiles as she took Pretzel's hand. Her blue silk dressing gown reminded Pretzel of the days she dressed up in Marthamum's clothes and she felt an immediate pang of guilt.

When Marika gazed intently into Pretzel's eyes, she gave a look of recognition.

"So, Prêtzova! You have arrived!"

"How did you know my name?"

She gave a secretive smile," I just knew in my bones."

Big Betty shook her head at Marika.

"Well. I said you two were of a kind. This girl is a fey one, also. The way she attracts the birdlife around her you'll both get on like a house on fire no doubt."

Marika hugged her friend. "My dear, the three of us can share our tales. No one is left out in this house..... Well, you sailoresses, I have lamb and onion patties, the best new tender spinach from my garden, and you must sample my blackberry wine. I've been waiting for a visitor to share it for it is not meant to be drunk alone."

The wine was warm and syrupy and after the meal, Big Betty spread herself out on the couch and was soon snoring loudly.

Marika took Pretzel's hand. "My dear, I know your friend."

"Which friend is that?"

Marika began to hum.

"You mean... Harragar?"

"She is a wise one that. She guessed you would meet me on your journey."

"But how could you have you talked with her? Her home will be deep in snow."

"I have friends like yours."

"Big Betty knows nothing about Harragar and I haven't dared mention the ..."

"Wattoo?"

Pretzel had instinctively avoided mentioning the word to any one since she had left the mountain. Here at last was a fellow human being she could hope to share her experiences with.

"Life's winds blow we know not how or where. Our generous friend here refuses to believe in the other world, but she is so close to it she fears it even more. I love my old friend and more for the fact even if she does not know things, she feels her way into them anyway."

Pretzel went to the window and looked at the port lit up below.

"Marika! Do you also know about my bird friends?"

"No, I do not, for they must be your soul creatures. I have my own that you will see in the morning but you will not be able to hear what they say."

"Did you climb the mountain too?"

Big Betty stirred and sat up. "You see! You two whispering together already while I sleep! I've had my forty winks now so I can sit out most of the night with you Marika, and I've been hoping you will travel back with me tomorrow."

"Come, Pretzel, you must be tired. I will show you your room."

Pretzel was impressed by Marika's diplomacy. She sat on her bed listening to the loud voice of Big Betty followed by the joyful laughter of Marika, glad of some time to herself so she could gather her thoughts together. She wished Betty hadn't woken when she did so she could confide in Marika her uncertainty what next she must do, but it wasn't to be. She looked out to see Roland perched on the fence in the moonlight. He flew over as soon as she beckoned him.

"What now?"

"You all must be enjoying a good feed but be careful not to get caught. Tell the others that tomorrow we will meet again. I will see the two women off and then we can begin our travels together…on land you will all be relieved to know. Give bird kisses to the wingflits and sleep well."

"The Bettina," chirped Roland, before flying back to the port.

Pretzel smiled to herself, "He always is of such few words."

She lay awake listening to the sounds of the port mingled with the wind which buffeted the cottage throughout the night. In the early hours of the morning a fog horn echoed around the harbour, and she shivered with delight at the newness of that deep throb that carried with it sea tales long past. As dawn broke she could hear Big Betty's snoring and tiptoed out to find Marika surrounded by butterflies: There were large ones with bronze wings the span of a child's hand, others that were deep emerald with red dots on their bodies, while the majority had lemon co-loured wings the size of a grain of rice. They filled the air giving the appearance of dancing lights. She watched Marika whisper-ing to them when they alighted on her hands.

"Meet my butterflies. I am so fortunate they came to me when I was lost and alone."

Pretzel sat down cautiously to avoid crushing them.

"They are wondrous…Marika, but I must ask you. Did you carry the Vordak pebbles from the mountain?"

"Yes. I did."

"Do you open them often?"

"In the beginning all the time but now, no longer."

"Why is that?"

"You too will find out one day."

"You speak in riddles like Harragar."

"No. I am not another Harragar. She is not like either of us but the day will come when…"

Betty staggered out, her eyes squinting in the light.

"Oh here you two are, gassing away. You and your butterfly mates! It's a wonder I need to be here at all! We must hurry to leave for the tide is on its way in and will turn at noon. I've at last convinced Marika to come back for the spring."

Marika held out her hand to Pretzel.

"I wish that I could have spent more time with you my dear."

Pretzel's heart sank as she couldn't help feeling abandoned again. When Big Betty went inside, Marika hugged Pretzel.

"But I want to talk to you more. There is so much I want to ask…"

"You have seen more than most, and we both understand each other. That is the greatest gift we both can have."

Pretzel sadly repacked and together the three of them walked single file down the hill until they were met by the same two boys who offered to carry their bags in exchange for coins.

"That is where the carriage leaves for Rossenduk. You will have plenty of time to see the Bettina off and return to catch it."

Big Betty noticed Pretzel looking anxiously up at the silos.

"They will have flown off by now in search of food and nests. They would not stick around you for ever. They are wild things you know."

Marika winked at Pretzel.

"Aright you two! I know I am odd one out all blather and not understanding."

When they reached the boat it was heaving and groaning on the ropes.

"It'll be a rough trip back this time but look at her! She can't wait to be out on the open sea. Well my Little Betty- Pretzel, I am going to miss you despite your funny ways."

Big Betty buried her in her arms and saturated her hair with tears before turning quickly and walking over to the boat. Marika kissed her on both cheeks before following Big Betty. Pretzel stood waving until her arm felt if could drop off. When the women's overcoats were just two red specks, she turned back to meet the wingflits, hoping they would soon cheer her out of her melancholy.

*

Drako sat fishing, enjoying the first warm day of spring and listening to the occasional croak. As he looked into the deep green water it suddenly became darker and looked up to see if a cloud had come over but there was none. When he looked down again the lake became a mass of swirling colours.

"I need to eat, I'm getting whoozy."

He packed up his gear and turned to look at the lake again. This time he was convinced he could make out the face of his sister. He looked down at P.D and at the gaps where the topaz once were.

"We are about to change the village rules, for if they won't let me keep you, I go too."

CHAPTER 22   ROSSENDUK

When Pretzel returned towards the silos, Roland flew down to meet her.

"The carriage is leaving for Rossenduk and then you can follow it. I can't wait before I can be with you all again, away from these onlookers as I stand out like a…lost parrot."

Roland chirped a farewell before disappearing into the roof of the silo. She assumed that Tachymus had advised them to remain well out of sight, for they had learned the hard way that humans killed birds to protect their grain.

The carriage was gaily painted with intricate patterns but all the same Pretzel felt a lump in her throat as she watched it fill up with children. They all sported the same deep blue jacket with Port Prohsorm School embossed on the pocket. They brushed past her as they fought for the best seats. Up till now, Pretzel had put any idea of school out of her mind but now felt a wave of nausea. Tears welled up in her eyes as she climbed up before finding a place at the back. When she leant out of the window to see the wingflits assembling in the trees, she felt calmer. At first, none of the school children noticed them as they were too intent on making cheeky comments at the driver who cranked up the engine before stepping in.

When they reached the top of the hill with its view down to the Port, Pretzel could make out a boat heading towards Rock Trishk and recognized the familiar shape of the sails. She felt a momentary pang until she remembered Domto. No way would she consider returning to Bettysville and face him despite the women's hospitality.

The children chattered loudly and ignored Pretzel. She felt much less conspicuous in the dress that Marika had given her. She leant against the window trying to relax but felt more and more confused. Her flags were no longer with her to guide her, but whenever she broke open a pebble it indicated she was to return. She would be the first Gratacian ever to return home and there would be so many questions and wondered how she would answer. Part of her wished to be famous as she knew she would be, but another part of her wanted to remain invisible. She broke open a Vordak pebble which revealed Marthamum, Poppo and Drako sitting by their little goat herd, and her fear turned into excitement as she realized she only need to break one open and show then and they would all be in raptures. The pebbles would explain everything. She felt soothed by their warmth in her hand and closed her eyes until she realized she was being spoken to.

"Eh Miss! What's your name?"

"Little Bet…Pretzel."

A boy whose knuckles were covered in a sea of warts offered her gum.

"Where are you going?"

"To Rossenduk."

"You live there?"

"No. Grataco"

"What is Grataco?"

"It is my town on the other side of the mountains."

"Never heard of it."

"You wouldn't as no one ever ventures…"

She stopped herself as she thought better than to explain the strange customs of her folk.

"How will you get there?"

"Walk."

The boys turned to look at her in surprise and she quickly changed the subject.

"So where are all of you traveling to?"

"The other side of Rossenduk, for a picnic."

The air felt cooler as the bus continued to climb. Pretzel felt her ears pop as she chewed her gum. When she watched the children comfortably chatting together she again felt another tinge of panic for she realized she would be expected to start back at school and live the same life as before.

"Strange," Pretzel thought to herself, "I never thought I would feel more afraid to return than I was to leave."

When she swiveled round to see the wingflits following, her spirits lifted. It was a winding road up to Rossenduk and with each turn she could see Roland in front leading the way. Eventually they did not escape the notice of the school children who had been instructed to draw trees and wildlife as they went along. Out came the coloured pencils. Pretzel was intrigued to see their pages showing yellow beaks and black wings with flashes of that startling green. She was enthralled at their representations but there were no Batwins. It would take an observant school child to detect his domed beak amongst them all.

"Have you seen these birds before?" she asked the boy with the warts.

"I'm not to know. Don't do any bird watching."

An earnest looking boy chimed in, "They must have migrated from the south. It has been a particularly cold winter," as he continued recording their details in his book.

Pretzel was intrigued that wherever she had traveled, no one recognized them as having seen them before.

The driver stopped at the top of a hill, allowing his passengers to clamber out to stretch their legs and survey the view while the wingflits perched in the trees above. The hills were mauve in the distance, and to the east one taller peak seemed to her as if it was pointing the way to Grataco. This time Pretzel's legs began to shake.

When the bus started up again, the boys attention was now fully on the wingflits.

"Look at that! They're following us again. Hey lady! Is it you they are following!"

Pretzel was about to shake her head, but suddenly felt tired of all this pretence and no one had ever called her 'lady' before. What did she have to lose? She was parting company when they reached Rossenduk anyway.

"Yes, they are actually. They befriended me and now they follow me everywhere."

Two boys kept nudging each other and looking round at her, while Pretzel felt uncomfortable at suddenly becoming a celebrity.

"My dad shoots the ones that eat our corn," said one off handedly.

"These won't."

But Pretzel remembered Harragar waving the birds off her trees. After all they were birds.

"If your father ever sees these birds, please tell him not to shoot them. I will make sure they won't eat your crops."

The bus wound on past succulent tree ferns and swathes of creepers covered in orange daisies. It was obvious to Pretzel that the rain was much heavier than in Grataco where it sat on the lee side of the mountains. The ground here was mossy green and velvety and very different from her own landscape with its bald mountain crags.

The bus driver tooted his horn as he approached Rossenduk. The road into town was lined with an avenue of tall poplars, casting shadow stripes on the brown earth as the bus flashed by. It drew to a halt outside the markets and Pretzel waved to the boys as it took off again. She looked up at the poplars to see the wingflits reassemble before flying into the undergrowth for shelter. She sat on the wooden seat to collect her thoughts before taking out the coins Big Betty had given her in payment for the boat.

The market square was alive with women carrying brightly coloured woven baskets. Pretzel merged among them in Marika's dress so no one paid her any attention. There was an abundance of fruit and vegetables, together with artichokes as big as footballs. She would have loved to have spent her money on those, but instead settled for the dried apricots, dates and nuts to fill her cocoon sac, for she knew she could not continue to rely on her good luck to find food wherever she had been. She had no idea if there would be any farmhouses in the mountain passes.

She was keen to make the most of daylight so hurried on past the saw mill on the outskirts, where a few of the workers stopped their work to stare at her. As soon as she was in open country she changed back into Reza's pyjamas for the long grass tickled her legs. The wingflits soon rejoined her and with Sorro flapping about her with glee, wished this moment would last forever.

The ground was scattered with plenty of rocks to use as stepping stones for the long grass reminded her that the snakes would be waking from their winter sleep, and she broke off a stick to pound on the rocks to frighten them.

"We will keep watch," Tachymus stated earnestly.

"How many walkers have a bird or two to keep and eye out for dangers like these?" Pretzel laughed.

Many days passed, for the mountains are always further away than they seem, but Pretzel didn't care for she was

193

deliriously happy. The sun warmed her back by day and her co-coon sac kept her warm at night. The wingflits sheltered in the trees above. It had been so idyllic that she had almost forgotten her Vordak Pebbles until one night she remembered and broke one open. She saw Drako stroking his possum dog, and he was crying, burying his face in the fur. She saw her family watching her with curiosity as she arrived surrounded by her wingflits and she tried to put them out of her mind in order to sleep but it was futile.

"Tachymus. I will need to gather you all together to explain to the fledglings how they should behave when we reach Grataco."

Tachymus nodded solemnly. Pretzel noted his chest puffed up and guessed he was glad of the opportunity to show his leadership skills again, for Batwin's topaz retrieving skills had put him out of the limelight. He flew into a cave that fitted Pretzel and most of the birds, while the remainder perched in small prickle bushes that would ward off predators from above and below. As soon as the chirping and fluttering s had settled down, Tachymus spoke.

"Hear our friend out."

"Out out out," twittered the winglets, and he had to hold his wings open until they had quietened down.

"My beloved wingflits! We will soon be approaching my home. It has been a whole year that we have been together and I have been too afraid to ask you this question. Now what will happen? Where will you go? Will you be returning to where you came from or are you staying with me?"

"We are all still here, still here," they replied in unison.

"Yes I know you all are still here and I am so happy, but it would be selfish of me to ask you to remain with me for ever."

Freya put her beak to Pretzel's ear.

"I will never go."

"But I am worried what may happen if the Gratacians think you are after their crops."

Tachymus shook his head.

"Not so, not so."

"Why are you are so sure they will not treat you all as foreign birds and chase you away?"

"You will see."

There appeared to be no more discussion so Pretzel decided to change the subject.

"I have to practice being ordinary again, and if my folk see me talking to you they will not believe my stories. They do not speak our language and not only that, I have to wear the long dress and no longer be seen in Reza's pyjamas for this village has a lot of rules and they wont listen to me if they see me as too odd. It is very sad I know."

"Sad and silly, sad and silly."

"Quiet, Sorro. Let her speak."

"I will have to go back to school and all of you will have to be seen as birds. Fly into trees, chirp in birdlike fashion and avoid strangers."

"Sad time, such a sad time."

"No, Freya. We will all still be together. I will take frequent walks out of Grataco. Then we can sit and talk as we are now. I will work something out, you will see. Anyway, tonight we are having a party!"

Pretzel brought out the special birdseed bought at the markets which she had kept for emergencies. She scattered them on the floor of the cave and while the wingflits pecked around her, she opened her last packet of apricots. When they had all had their fill, Pretzel jumped up and began to dance. She spun and spun, while the winglets copied her movements flying in circles around her. Pretzel laughed and shrieked, until she fell in a heap.

"Oh, if Harragar could see us all now! We will do lots more of this whenever we can, I promise you!"

"Lots, lots, lots."

"Never leave you never leave you."

But when Pretzel lay in the dark, she had her doubts that Batwin really would remain in Grataco. He could well want to return to the Mountains of Tarzon with Freya. There were so many pressing things on her mind that she slept only in small increments, until she dreamt yet again of her brother, his possum dog, and a collar studded with topaz that then disappeared one by one leaving gaps like missing teeth.

She sat up with a start.

"Batwin?"

There was no reply.

CHAPTER 23   THE HOMECOMING

On the morning of the Springfest, Drako brushed his dog down with mixed feelings. He had dreamt of showing him off to the audience and surprising them, his parents included, with the stones, but after the last three were taken he felt there was little point. He still planned to read the poem that he had written about his sister, but had so badly wanted to include the story about his dog and had hoped the topaz could be used to buy P.D. back from the village. After much deliberation he decided to tell the story in any case and the audience would just have to think it was his imagination talking.

"You don't care one scrap, do you P.D.?" he said as he patted him.

His heart ached for his sister on this special day, and he now had extreme pangs of guilt for having preferred she stay away so he could keep the dog. He reluctantly took out his celebratory silk shirt and struggled with the buttons, glad that Marthamum had let out the seams for his shoulders had broadened considerably. The stiff embossed leather belt that Poppo had given to him carried off the red shirt and black trousers to perfection.

"I will be taller than Pretzel now, P. D."

He went to the window and looked down at the valley. Already people from the surrounding villages were spilling out from gaily painted buses, but the excited yells from children echoing round the square just made him more miserable. He was about to turn away when a flash of green appeared on he window sill. It was the same bird that had left all those months ago with the stone in its beak. He knew that because of its strange worn down shape.

"You could have returned at least one of them!"

"Drako, who is there?"

"No one, Marthamum. I am practicing my poem."

Marthamum tried on one scarf after the other, but nothing seemed to match.

"Come and help me, Drako! Poppo doesn't know these things. You are better with colour."

Drako went in to her bedroom and hugged his mother as tears fell down her cheeks.

"I want my Pretzi to be here so badly."

She held him by the shoulders looking into his face.

"Son. You haven't heard the call also, have you?"

"No, Marthamum. I would block my ears from them if they dared try…But she is not ever coming back is she! No one ever does! Why didn't you stop her?"

"That is the Gratacian way, dear son. Remember that."

"Then you are a brave and wonderful mother to trust Pretzel and not follow after her."

By the time Drako returned to his room the bird was gone.

*

There was much panic squawking when the wingflits woke to find Batwin missing. Pretzel was relieved that there were no telltale feathers lying around as Roland flew above trying to spot him from the sky.

"You must not fret, Freya. He will be safe somewhere. He knows how to avoid danger."

"I will stay here till he returns."

Pretzel stroked Freya's head.

"Freya, Batwin will return, I promise you. He is too smart to get himself eaten. He will find us along the path but I must reach Grataco before nightfall. They will be sitting down to dinner and I will surprise them. I can't wait to see the look on their faces!"

"Tidy up," called Tachymus.

Pretzel smiled despite her concerns. How she loved watching him organizing them all.

By the time Pretzel reached the last summit, it was late afternoon. There were no trails leading to Grataco for they had been obliterated by landslides from the winter snows. She decided to take a direct route straight down the mountain side, which meant much scrambling down mud slides. She took in the view of her village in the distance, her excitement at returning now dampened as there was still no sign of Batwin.

*

Batwin had guessed how much the boy had marveled at the stones, for all birds love bright things. He knew Pretzel needed them for her survival, but as the group had neared Grataco he thought of the boy and how sad he must have been to have them stolen in front of his very nose and the fact he did not even harm the birds, he must be a friend. He decided that he must fly off to the caves immediately to the finest of all the topaz he had remembered seeing. The wind was in the right direction and he flew with speed to chisel it out, delighting in his favourite pastime and singing when he needed to rest frequently. At last it was in his beak. It had the smoothest of edges and when he carried it out to the sunlight he could see it had a rare brilliance. He rested with it outside the cave until he gathered his strength to return to Grataco.

*

Poppo had been up with the goats all day, leading them to higher ground, which was now free of snow. Already their shaggy coats were beginning to thin. But today he was in a hurry. Marthamum had insisted he be home early to dress for the Festival. He had polished his boots in readiness, but did not appreciate how his feet felt, pressed and pummeled to fit into them, but it was important to give comfort to his wife. She was so unhappy without her daughter to preen and dress up for the occasion. Poppo patted his goats and turned to leave down the mountain.

*

Distances are illusionary. Pretzel saw a speck in the distance that she was sure had to be Poppo. She felt she could run down the mountain and surprise him, but there were deep gullies to negotiate. She had slipped enough, each time Reza's pyjamas becoming more caked with mud. She could not chance a broken leg.

'That isn't the Gratacian way either,' she muttered, "Gratacian way Gratacian way! How much this dominates my thinking already!"

*

Late afternoon Drako could hear the sound of accordions floating up from the Square. He smoothed down his black springy hair with oil and pulled back his shoulders to admire his frame in the mirror, together with P.D. now brushed to a golden sheen.

"You need a feed before we go."

He led him outside and stepped back with surprise. The same bird that he had seen at the window flew down and deposited a stone beside the feeding bowl before flying up the valley.

He turned the topaz round in his hands. It was warm, smooth and had a glow that made up for the missing six. It gave him solace as he set it well into the collar, covering it over with P.D.'s fur.

"You will be mine for ever, PD."

Poppo, dressed in his neat grey trousers and emerald green jacket, walked gingerly in his boots.

"Come on. The three of us and PD. Drako, you do know it is a year gone and he must be returned to the Square."

"I do know that, Poppo."

This time to his parents' relief, he did not appear so bothered. They linked arms before waving to Reza who was bedecked in bright turquoise silk, the latest of the colours from her vats.

*

Pretzel slipped down the last gully that led to where the goats were grazing, but Poppo was nowhere to be seen so she assumed he had turned for home early. She looked down at her mud splattered pyjamas.

"They may not want to know the new Pretzel."

"We like you," Freya chimed in.

"Thank goodness I have you all, my special friends but, if only…"

Before she had a chance to mention Batwin's name, he landed amongst them.

"I told you Freya, he would be back."

As the wingflits crowded round Batwin, Tachymus warned them to stay clear of the villagers who would see them as a threat to their crops. They chirped a farewell to Pretzel before flying off into the grove where they were soon well hidden from view.

Pretzel ran towards the house past the little stone wall which she touched with her fingers, feeling their familiar afternoon warmth where she had sat on them swinging her legs a lifetime ago. There was no smoke coming from the chimney so guessed Marthamum must be busy preparing the stove in readiness to light. She peered through the kitchen window to see the table set out with the dishes in readiness for the next meal. There were three places and she felt a sudden bolt of pain in her chest, realizing how dreadful it must have been for all of them and she pulled open the back door trying not to cry.

"I must not show I am sad. I must look my best. They must be proud of me. They must listen to my story from beginning to end and when they see what the pebbles reveal they will no longer be sad."

There were none of the usual cooking aromas as she walked in.

"Marthamum, Poppo, Drako!"

She wandered through to the front garden feeling a quiver of fear. She noted her favourite pine tree, the irises taking bud, and that life seemed to have gone on as usual without her. As she stood watching the sky become deep mauve, wondering all manner of disasters that may have befallen them, she heard the sound of musicians and hurried down the path to see people converging onto the Village Square all in their finery. She looked down at her mud-splattered pyjamas but was beyond caring.

The villagers were quickly seated, clapping noisily and shouting as the fiddlers from Lafaz had yet again begun to excite the crowd. No one noticed her arrival as the audience was engrossed in the drummers, clowns, acrobats and children on stilts. There were the usual choir madrigals, puppet theatre, comedy acts and skits until high above them a young girl spun around and around on a red silk curtain, followed by the final performance on the trapeze.

'Nothing has changed,' Pretzel thought to herself as she stood at the back in the shadows.

The musicians were about to pack up their instruments when suddenly, out from the wings of the stage, walked Drako followed by his possum dog. He took out his scroll, facing the town leaders who were seated in the front row and began to recite his poem.

> "I had a sister once who went away
> To far off lands and distant seas.
> I can no longer say her name
> For the words of Grataco state,
> She is no longer part of our world.
>
> I have a dog, his name is PD
> He is my comfort all these days.
> One whole year and now I grieve
> For I must return him back
> And my heart breaks.
>
> But watch now all and you will see
> A collar with a wondrous stud
> A topaz here as brilliant as the sun
> For this is payment for my dog to keep.
> For he is worth more than a thousand mines."

With that Drako smoothed the fur back to display the topaz as the audience sat in stunned silence.

"Keep the dog boy. Keep the dog," people called as he knelt and buried his face in P. D's fur.

When Drako stood up, he noticed a young woman standing at the back of the hall. She looked so like his sister despite her strange attire. He stepped off the stage and walked down the aisle to take a closer look as the audience craned their necks and watched with amazement as Drako held her and rocked her, dancing round and round soon joined by Marthamum and Poppo. Pretzel was home.

CHAPTER 24   THE PEBBLES OF VORDAK

The band from Lafaz continued to play throughout the night as the old folk unabashedly touched Pretzel to satisfy themselves that she was real. The acrobats carried out more and more daring manoevres high above the stage while the clowns juggled every object they could lay their hands on, causing whoops of laughter as hats, scarves and shoes flew into the air. The villagers danced until dawn threw a purple glow over the mountains. Only then they staggered home, leaving behind upturned picnic baskets, discarded shawls and a wake of boots dropped hither and thither as the dancing had become increasingly wild. Poppo, drunk with the new season's wine and delirious with joy, needed to be helped home between Drako and Marthamum. Pretzel walked alongside this tottering threesome, feeling overwhelmed that her arrival had created such an impact and half wished she had landed into someone else's celebration.

Marthamum steered Pretzel to her bed and sat trying to untangle her matted hair as tears rolled down her plump cheeks. Poppo stuck his head round the door, and then quickly disappeared outside, blowing his nose loudly.

"Poppo drunk too much before you arrived. He couldn't bear the thought of going to the Lake Fest with all those memories of the night you left. We women have to be strong and manage some how. It has been so hard Prêtzova... and now here you are beyond your old mother's wildest dreams with your father being the worse for wear.

Drako stood at the foot of Pretzel's bed, his beloved dog nuzzling his shin.

"I'm taller than you now."

"I'm browner than you, brother."

Pretzel leaned forward to inspect the stone in P.D'S collar as Drako gave her a quizzical look.

"I have so much to tell you, but I can't keep awake any longer."

She collapsed back onto the softest bed she had lain on for a year and fell asleep immediately. The velvet night was absent of dreams, and the next day half passed before she stirred. She woke to the familiar aroma of leek and chicken soup, the dish she had most missed on her journey, and wandered in to the kitchen.

"Look how thin you have become." Marthamum exclaimed, rubbing her daughter's lean shoulders. "And your skin is like leather. All that hot sun. Let me wash your hair now."

Pretzel laid her head back in the basin allowing her mother to pour the warm water over her hair. When Marthamum massaged her scalp, she closed her eyes to hide her tears at feeling a small child again.

Over lunch Pretzel drew a rough guide to show them how far she had traveled. She began to relate her adventures, but was interrupted by so many questions she became confused, and when she tried to explain her communication with the wingflits, she stopped again wondering if perhaps she had made it all up for they stared at her uncomprehendingly.

"You mean, those birds really had a conversation with you?"

"Yes. They are very unusual birds. They have never been seen in these parts."

She started to wonder if she was talking about a dream she had until Drako exclaimed, "Except I saw one too, Poppo."

"Where?"

"At the window and later when it dropped the topaz by PD's dinner bowl."

"Did it talk to you?"

"No, not at all, but they were the ones that stole the stones out of PD's collar because I saw the feathers."

"But the birds didn't talk to you, did they?"

Pretzel wished she had not spoken of her friends for she knew if she continued on in this manner, Poppo would get the village doctor. How could she explain her rescue by Batwin if no one would believe her? She went on to describe the desert, and the Catoa that supplied her with nourishment but avoided mentioning the quicksand for it would have terrified them to think of the manner in which she would have died but for Batwin. No, it was better to limit her tale to what they could make sense of. It was easier to talk of Saraden City and how no one was allowed to be unhappy until Marthamum sighed.

"Oh how wonderful! You must have liked meeting those people!"

"No Marthamum. It was horrible."

"Why dear?"

"Because they were punished if they were sad."

She decided to leave out her tales of escape from the hospital and went on to describe Harragar.

"She must have been like a grandmother to you," murmured Marthamum, showing relief that her daughter at last had met a person not unlike one of the elderly Gratacians.

They sat in awe as Pretzel went on to describe her climb over the mountain passes and how she kept clear of the wild beasts while Poppo nodded approvingly.

" And then I climbed Mt Vordak."

"And how high is this mountain?"

"High enough to run out of breath easily so I needed to go slowly…and then I…I jumped, I mean I climbed down into a canyon so dark…"

"But you were so alone!" Marthamum cried, "My poor little daughter!"

"Harragar knew I would be safe, and I had Freya…"

"Who is Freya?"

"One of the wingflits… birds. I rescued her from a cage in Saraden city."

By this time Marthamum and Poppo were giving her the strangest of looks, but Pretzel no longer cared.

" She waited for me until I came back from the Wattoo."

Pretzel clapped her hand over her mouth but it was too late.

"The what?"

Poppo's face darkened and his knees began to shake uncontrollably as he stared into his daughter's face.

"And then?" he asked in a whisper.

She felt for her Vordak pebbles and hesitated, relieved to hear a knock at the door. Reza entered carrying a lemon cake and a bundle of silk. She kissed Pretzel on both cheeks.

"You would be grown out of your clothes by now. When you have time I will measure you."

Reza pointed to the well-worn pyjamas hanging on the line, while Pretzel blushed, thinking how fast her journey was fading, just as those pyjamas were. She put on a gracious smile at Reza's gentle teasing but when Reza eventually left, she felt pinned to the wall by her father's intense expression.

Pretzel took a deep breath, feeling she was confronting the Wattoo all over again.

"What was it?"

Pretzel remembered Harragar's warning about those that will not understand and will lock her away, but it was too late. She felt compelled to go on.

"It was a sort of …pool, and then it became a hole and then it was black and then the palest of blue and then all colours of the world and I went down and I have found these….

"I hope you didn't risk your life climbing down into it with no one to rescue you if you fell," Marthamum interrupted.

"No you mustn't fall. You jump....And anyway I 'm here aren't I?"

Poppo went pale, shaking his head in disbelief. The feeling soon passed and his familiar mood returned.

"I thought you were sensible."

"Then I floated down, and here. I have these."

"You floated!"

"See what I have brought home for you."

She reached into her pocket and showed one to Marthamum who turned it over in her hand.

"It feels very smooth and looks pretty, dear, but it is like the ones you find in the streams."

Pretzel broke one open and saw the face of Harragar who was smiling but also shaking her head.

"The pebbles re-form after they are broken. That is interesting." Poppo exclaimed, but he refused to inspect them too closely.

"Did you not see Harragar?"

The three looked nonplussed.

"Drako! Did you not see anything?"

Marthamum took her by the arm.

"My dear. You have eaten too much of that desert fruit, mixed with bad company, and who knows what that old woman was up to even though she was kind. Living out there on her own and all. Look at you now. Can't you see you have been talking with birds and seeing things that aren't there? She is not well Poppo! My poor little daughter!"

"She will be well soon Marthamum, I know and so does PD." Drako added, ruffling up her sister's hair.

Poppo looked at her with a longing that was too much to bear and a deep sadness that he was never to know of the riddles that his daughter spoke in, but again he shook himself out of his melancholy.

"Yes. Your sister will be back with us soon," he added hopefully.

"I have not gone anywhere. I am still here."

Pretzel stared out the window in dismay, feeling as if particles of glass had been thrown in her face. Not even her beloved Drako could see what the pebbles were revealing. It was too late now to heed Harragar's warnings. No one would ever take her seriously again.

"My dear you need rest. Lots of rest. I am going to feed you with our special soup from the malako and let you stay here quietly until you recover. Then you will be back at school and all will be as before."

Pretzel had no choice but to crawl into bed, pulling the covers over her. Her heart felt heavy as lead as she lay awake in spite of her exhaustion, fearing that her family believed she had really lost her mind and if that was the case she would be a source of their constant concern but also shame.

It was exactly a year since the thought flags had first arrived and now they were left behind in the Wattoo with none of them to encourage her and none of them advising her on where to turn next. She tried to keep her spirits up by breaking another pebble open, this time revealing the flags dancing peacefully in a circle without a care in the world.

"Too bad" she said to herself, "if no one can see what I can see. It just shows they are stupid. My family is just stupid."

But as the night went on her courage left her as she began to doubt herself again. If her brother could not see the images, no one in Grataco would, and Harragar was far away. She would have tossed and turned in despair all night had it not been for a feather light landing on her face.

"Sleep, Pretzi. Sleep."

"My little Freya," Pretzel whispered.

The bird watched her breaths deepening before flying away.

CHAPTER 25   THE SCHOOL AT LAFAZ

Pretzel woke just after dawn and looked out the window to see Poppo moving the new goat families up the mountain. She felt a pang as she wanted to kiss him before her left, to make sure he was real. She briefly felt a longing for the old Pretzel she was before but it was not to be. Marthamum heard her stir and carried in a bowl of hot porridge swimming in freshly made cream.

"You need to put on condition my girl."

"I am well, really I am! You are all treating me as if I am an invalid."

"My dear, no manner of things you have encountered, and look at the state you are in! You now can see why over the years most refuse to respond to their flags and who knows what happened to the ones that did for they never returned…"

"Marthamum! Just because you didn't listen to yours! You know I had to go. And I have returned so why scold me now. You all know very well the call of the flags, yet none of you want to know anything. You want to remain ignorant, that is your trouble, so I won't talk about it any more!"

Marthamum was silent for a while as she stroked her daughter's arm which stiffened under her hands. She decided to change the subject.

"And have you realized your new school starts in two weeks?"

Pretzel felt sick.

"I guessed it will. I don't want to go."

"My dear, we have struggled with your loss. You cannot imagine the strain and terror on our lives, never expecting to ever see you again and worst of all, not mentioning your name in public, just as if you did not exist. We all had to keep a brave face and obey the rules. And as for Drako, he needed much comfort."

"No he didn't! He had PD. He was more important."

"Pretzi! Have you returned more selfish? What happened to my nice little daughter? Any way the least you can do for Poppo is to go on with your education."

Pretzel sighed, "And what I have learned on my journey. Does not that count for anything?"

"It appears not."

Pretzel felt a knot in her belly. She wanted to run but where to? She just had to give in and gave a long sigh.

"Alright, Marthamum. I will go to school and try to fit in as best I can."

"My daughter, that is better. I will write a note explaining that you have been learning a lot of new things and will catch up as you are a bright girl."

Pretzel kissed her.

"Thank you Marthamum."

Pretzel made a supreme effort over the next two weeks to remember how she was before. She stopped opening her Vordak pebbles in the hope her family might believe she had returned to normality. But it did not take long before she could no longer bear keeping up her pretence. As soon as she was safe from her mother's scrutiny she took a walk out of town to meet with her beloved wingflits. Sorro collected tiny pink flowers in his beak to drop into Pretzel hair. She opened up her pebbles releasing images of crimson sunsets and mattresses bouncing down waterfalls.

"I can breathe again wingflits! I can't be lonely when I am with you."

The birds had found a massive pine tree well away from the usual mountain tracks and also perfect for nesting. After spending several hours with them Pretzel returned in a happier state of mind and Marthamum commented on the return of colour to her cheeks.

Pretzel's friends visited her often and pumped her with questions, but she was careful how to answer them.

"Pretzi, Pretz, you are so brave…but you are not one of us anymore".

She felt stung by their comments. It appeared to her that however hard she tried to be the Pretzel of old, they were seeing straight through her anyway.

"Then you will have to get used to me like this."

She appeared to them to make light of it, but inside she felt a stranger wherever she went. It was painful enough to see her precious brother looking at her oddly. However, at night when she opened her pebbles, she saw him standing by the Wattoo looking into the swirl of colours. She felt more comforted, knowing that the day might come when he may discover his own thought flags and find the need to follow a similar path, but it was obvious he was by no means ready yet and she admonished herself for expecting too much from him.

The day came sooner than she wished to face the new school year. She gathered together her good pencils, remembering that the ones from Lafaz broke easily. She polished her satchel until it was gleaming. Her long blue dress still felt strange on her despite two weeks of practice. Her hair already darker again from daily oiling was beginning to grow but not long enough to make plaits over her head. Marthamum helped secure it with ribbons, before preparing a packed lunch of bread and goats cheese.

Pretzel sat at the back of the bus to wait for her friends. Romela greeted her with a hug, Marko pulled at her ribbons and Dashika held Pretzel's hand all the way to the school of Lafaz which was situated in the outskirts of Grataco. When it pulled outside the imposing gates Pretzel gave a shudder.

"You can sit next to us in class," they all promised, understanding her discomfort.

Pretzel waved her mother's letter. "If the principal will let me stay."

"You haven't missed much. Anyway there will be a lot of those Lafaz kids in our class who are stupid. It must be the water," her friend giggled.

The teacher recognized Pretzel instantly as the girl that had been the centre of attention at the Springfest.

"What a homecoming! You are sure a one for the history books. A Gratacian who left and returned!"

To Pretzel's dismay, she was instructed to address the whole school about her journey. It was obvious by the teacher's attitude that she hoped that Pretzel would now have seen the folly of her ways and if anything, discourage others. She found herself in front of two hundred pairs of curious eyes and stammered her way through, telling them about the slippery tracks and wide rivers, the long desert trek, and her mountain climb. Questions followed.

"But weren't you scared?"

"What made you leave here?"

"How did you live in the desert and what did you eat?"

She went on to describe her ride on the boat to Port Prohsorm.

"Were you not afraid of the creatures of the deep?"

At last Pretzel could return to sit with her friend who patted Pretzel's arm. She hoped now she could fade into the background. She had deliberately not mentioned Harragar. A watered down version would not do the old woman proud.

At the morning break Pretzel asked her friend. "Why aren't you curious to see what I have seen for yourselves?"

Marko took her aside. "You are foolhardy Pretz and discontented, that's all. We have everything here that we want, and look at you! You seem unhappier now than you have ever been."

"So you think all one needs is happiness?"

"Why on earth not, Pretz?"

"Have you never heard of curiosity?"

Pretzel knew for certain now that she could never slip back into their comfortable ways. She tried to listen to the Art Teacher, but after about ten minutes became increasingly fidgety and by lunchtime could stand it no longer.

"Tell Miss P. I am ill" she whispered to Dashika, "I need to go home."

"There is no bus."

"I can walk. It will take me about five hours which is nothing."

Dashika watched her hurry away as soon as the bell went.

'Pretz is no longer with us,' she later confided to Romela. "Perhaps she should never have returned."

Pretzel hurried past the students who were too engrossed in their lunch boxes to notice her pushing open the iron gates. When she reached the furthermost house she saw an old man weeding his vegetable patch. He stood up when he saw Pretzel and waved his blackened hand.

"Good day for walking. Glad they let you out early."

As soon as she was out of sight she collapsed onto a grassy hillock and looked up to see Freya.

"Pretzi, Pretzi, you are sad."

"I can't face going to school any more. It is like being in a cage."

Freya responded by giving a quiver at the word 'cage' before alighting on her shoulder to comfort her as the rest of the wingflits joined them.

Tachymus nodded his head earnestly. "Birds don't need to go to school."

"You know all you need to know. I miss Harragar's advice so much now. Only she understands."

She buried her face in her hands and cried while the wingflits kept a respectful distance. She eventually stopped and wiped her eyes.

"I have no choice but to go back to Harragar."

Batwin gave a worried sounding chirp.

"All the way back again?"

"Yes, that is the only thing to do."

"Just you?"

"No. All of us!"

Sorro hopped and somersaulted with glee down the incline, collecting moist grass on his feathers as they made their way back towards home, avoiding the road most of the way.

Pretzel arrived at her house not long after the bus had pulled up. She wasn't ready to explain herself, but already it was too late. The Gratacian grape vine had already reached Marthamum who stood anxiously waiting for her.

"I heard you were sick, my dear," but instead Pretzel had a glow about her that her mother hadn't seen since her return.

"I am not going back to Lafaz."

"So you really think school is not for you after all?"

Marthamum looked down at her own work worn hands with the torn fingernails, but was relieved that her daughter was at least looking back to normal.

"Well, I suppose we could do with more women to weave the rugs. And perhaps you can work and help Reza with her silk. And Poppo will be so happy if you join him. And it is time you learnt the art of Tabriz cooking as it is a dying art and I have dreamt of my daughter preparing the oven and us making the pastes together and… Look at your mother. I am happy and I didn't go to school. You will find a good village boy one day and settle down. You are pretty and it won't be hard with our help to find you the right husband. And the grandchildren…"

"I am off to see Reza now."

Marthamum was at first disgruntled as she was pulled out of her fantasies until she realized her daughter was behaving as a good neighbour should.

"That is thoughtful dear. She would like a visit."

Pretzel found Reza stirring beetroot juice into the vats and humming to her self at the thought of this season's crimson.

"Reza! I need some more pyjamas, just like the one you made for me before."

"But it is summer, my dear!"

Pretzel stood staring into the vats until Reza guessed what was afoot.

"Your mother…Does she know yet? What will she say?"

Pretzel fidgeted with a yellow shawl hanging over the chair.

"There is nothing she can say."

Reza took her by the shoulders. "That is the problem. That is why they never return. How I tried to warn you but it fell on deaf ears."

"Would it have made any difference?"

Reza bit her lip and sighed.

"Let's find some cloth then. This time yellow browns and greens. I'll make you a headscarf to go with it. And what about a new cocoon sac."

"No need. My red one is faithful. I won't abandon it."

Reza was beginning to enjoy their secret. "I won't tell a soul," she added.

Pretzel had to smirk. 'All of Grataco will know by midday tomorrow,' she thought to herself.

By the time she returned home, Drako was polishing his one large topaz which shone from P. D's collar. Poppo arrived soon after, stomping black earth out of his boots.

As Marthamum served out the pumpkin turnovers, Pretzel took a big sigh and stood up.

Her voice sounded determined as the three stared at her, not wanting to believe what she was telling them.

"I must return to Harragar."

"But daughter, you cannot…"

"She is old and may need me now."

As Pretzel predicted, they sat dumbfounded, but the explanation helped, for no Gratacian is left to die alone.

At last Pretzel could make an escape to her room. She could overhear Poppo trying to soothe her mother.

"She came back this time, remember. She knows this time she has broken the traditions and is free to return again and for good, mark my words."

"But Poppo my dear husband, she is no longer a normal Gratacian. How can you be so sure?"

Pretzel blocked her ears and opened a Vordak pebble to see Harragar climbing laboriously up the rope ladder to pick fresh berries, heard the ripple of her laughter and the rushing of the waterfall. She put them away and lay awake throughout the night listening to her mother's sobs and the low voice of Poppo comforting her. But when morning came, Marthamum and Poppo came in and sat beside her.

"It is the right thing to do. You must see to the old lady and if she is sick, you can bring her back with you to be cared for."

Pretzel hugged and held them both, feeling the rough hand of Poppo stroking the back of her neck.

"Harragar in Grataco?' she thought to herself, "I think not."

CHAPTER 26   RETURN TO HARRAGAR

None of the newest fledglings had experienced Harragar's berries, but the stories were legendary. They twittered with excitement unaware of the dangers awaiting them. Tachymus spent many a long night instructing them on how best to deal with the risks to a small bird and which they would soon see for themselves. Batwin and Freya had recently hatched three fine winglets of their own and they were full of pride for their brave parents as they listened spellbound.

*

Marthamum sat in her well-worn wicker chair spinning goat's wool alongside Poppo, who now spent most of his time at home to be with her. He had to gently warn Marthamum that this time they may lose their daughter for good for his wife was full of optimism.

"I know she has decided she must see to the old lady but she will return again this time," she had stated over and over again.

"But, Martha, we both know she isn't happy."

"We can ask her to promise…"

"No one can ask her to do that."

Marthamum pursed her lip. "I know the Gratacian refusal to force a promise. But look! Pretzel did return so… more than likely she will come back and bring Harragar with her."

"How will she carry her if she is too frail to cross the desert? Pretzel is a fit girl but not strong enough to carry her all that way."

"You are far too dismal I cannot bear it!"

"You must face the truth my dear that we have to part with her again and live with our not knowing."

For the rest of the afternoon they sat gazing down the valley in the direction where Pretzel would soon be leaving, aware that there was no chance of her changing her mind.

*

Drako trudged up the hill from school to meet Pretzel. She linked her arm through his.

"We must talk."

They sat together in Drako's bedroom. Pretzel fondled P.D.'s ears and cleared her throat.

"I know you won't wish to do this, but there is something I must ask of you."

"You want me to come too?"

"No, Drako! But I have another ask, a big one. I…I need to …take your topaz."

Drako looked crestfallen.

"I know. I am sorry. It is so special… but it will be put to good use and it also may buy…."

"What is there to buy out in the desert, Pretz?"

"There is much I haven't told you, as I tried to describe to our parents what happened to me in Saraden City but I gave up as they didn't want to know anything bad."

Pretzel related how the citizens appeared at first to be living a charmed life, but were never permitted to leave the walls. She told him of her lucky escape using a stone of Tarzon, and hoped this one may buy freedom for her friends, Larrida and Tarod.

"You can't mean you will go back in there!"

"Do not worry your head. I would never do that."

"Then how will you give it to them?"

"I will think of something. I will find another way for I will never again enter those gates for all the delicious food smells in the world...The topaz. It is settled, then?"

Drako wrestled with himself and sighed," Settled, Pretz. You have my word."

Pretzel hugged her brother who had tears in his eyes and who was feeling a tinge of guilt at feeling the loss of his stone more than the separation from his sister.

Drako ruffled PD's neck.

"I guess we'll manage without it. At least I have you and you don't care."

*

Pretzel needed weeks to plan and equip herself for her journey. This time she knew what lay in front of her and she puzzled over this: How the journey into the unknown needs little planning, but now that she knew what was ahead, there were all manner of considerations. It was easier in that she could work out what she needed to supplement her food supply, and harder as she no longer had the naivety and optimism she had before. Too many dangers she now knew could happen along her path, but the thought of seeing Harragar again boosted her courage.

She visited the shoemaker and asked for slippers with feathers on the soles. Drako looked at her strangely.

"I need them if the nights are cold."

She gathered up seeds for the wingflits, for this time they would be following her into the desert and they would not be expected to relish the Catoa. She packed dried apricots, raisins, and cured meat in thick spicy paste. She made sure to pack a notepad and pencil that worked. When she visited the Jarrod the canoe maker, she drew him a design out of a square piece of canvas and showed where the flaps were to be, with edging to insert bamboo poles.

"The canvas must be well waterproofed."

"Wouldn't you rather a sturdy wooden canoe?"

"This needs to be carried a long distance."

He said nothing as all of Grataco was now commiserating with Marthamum and Poppo on the strange behaviour of their daughter.

When Pretzel returned two weeks later to collect it she was thrilled with the outcome.

"It is so light!"

He watched Pretzel leave jubilantly with her package, shaking his head.

*

Reza completed Pretzel's pyjamas with a flourish, and re-lined her cocoon sac.

"How does your family bear to see you leave again? You are too cruel!"

"Please Reza. Don't you give me hard time as well!" The villagers won't look at me now they have wind that something is afoot. I am no longer trusted and they stay away from me when I go down into the town as they may catch my … disease."

Reza took Pretzel's arm. "I have never told you this. My flags used to visit me often and showed me the way out of Grataco also. They pressured me day and night."

"You refused to follow them?"

Reza's voice became low and sad. "I nearly did. I packed my things and was going to slip away but I was too afraid. I thought of long dark nights alone and ... so here I am for ever with my vats. "\

"But, you could still..."

"It is too late. We will speak no more of it Pretzi. You see I envy you too much."

Pretzel could get no further word from Reza who moved away to at the window. She stood staring down into the valley.

"Go now, but ... please return for all our sakes."

"You know you can't ask that of me."

"I know too well."

Pretzel felt any further conversation was futile, so returned home to find Marthamum boiling up a large supply of grape and fig jam.

"You must take this to the old lady."

Pretzel kissed her mother, for she knew now the brave face she was putting on.

*

For all of the final week, Pretzel's family spent sitting around the table late into the night. To any of the villagers looking through the window, it would have seemed a celebration of Pretzel's return yet they knew the rumours and signs were otherwise.

Old Varsla had refused to visit her granddaughter, When Marthamum and Poppo brought over the newly spun shawl she took her daughter in law's arm. "You see my son turned into a good man and stayed at home to look after me, not like his father."

Marthamum stared at her in amazement and then at Poppo.

"You all told me he had died falling off the cliff!"

"He could well have done...You see the rest of the village girls are angels. They all stay at home and look after the old folk."

Marthamum could on longer stand it.

"Well. Our girl is different. I don't want to hear any more of these 'stay at homes'," she eventually exploded, trying to suppress her tears as Poppo's jaw dropped, looking at his wife with a mixture of pride and surprise.

*

At last Pretzel was ready. She chose the night, hoping to tiptoe out of her village but this time it was not possible. As she trudged down the hill with her load on her back, she turned around to wave to her family on the cliff, silhouetted by the moon, but curious people in their hordes loomed out of the darkness. She couldn't help feeling they were all in attendance at her funeral.

"Take care of the topaz, Pretz," Drako called.

She heard one voice cry out, "You're stupid and selfish," and guessed it belonged to Varsla who over the past week had still refused to talk to her.

Pretzel started to cry, but when she reached the lake where she met up with her wingflits, Sorro cheered her up with his antics. Soon she was laughing again with Freya who twittered softly in her ear as of old.

As morning appeared, they arrived at the place where Roland had divined the water with his beak. It all seemed so simple now as she watched the birds drink and bathe in the spring.

"What of the Hetzenbabel, Roland?"

"Very big now. Longer claw."

Pretzel produced her feather slippers which the wingflits eyed curiously.

"It will save me having to tread on all your tail feathers."

When they reached the Hetzenbabel, the stench was foul, but there was no sign of the sad creature.

"I feel sorry for the monster cooped up for ever." she whispered. "Not that I intend to rescue it all the same."

She was able to appreciate the beauty of the cliffs when they were well out of danger. The winglets were keen to explore every nook and cranny in the rocks, but when it was time to cross the desert, Tachymus gathered them all together to warn them.

"You must stay on the path whenever you land, for the there are patches of the desert that is either quicksand or bird eating. We do not want to lose any of you."

Pretzel demonstrated how she calmed the shimmers down by feeding them Catoa, and when it was their time to feed, to perch in a queue along the path as she threw them their seeds.

She chuckled at the picture of it as they began their crossing and she marveled at how Tachymus kept them all in check as they traveled past the shimmers without incident.

As soon as Saraden city was in view, this time it was Freya who addressed the wingflits, warning them not to fly over the walls despite the promise of a good feed.

As for Pretzel, the smell of soup was even more delicious and she stuffed he mouth with Catoa and blocked her nose to stave off the tantalizing aroma. When she reached the Western Wall, she pulled out her pad and pencil.

"Now, what?" asked Batwin.

"I have another task for you, Batwin. See that tower that is closest to us. In there lives a lady who has long grey hair plaited down her back just like Marthamum, and she wears a pinafore, which is as blue as Lake Grataco. Her name is Larrida. She has a husband and three boys…"

"Larrida Larrida Larrida."

"Be quiet, winglets!"

"I am writing a letter for you to take to her."

Pretzel jotted a note, "Dear Larrida and Tarod, I am camped on the western path not far from your tower. When you receive this, wave from your window and my friend Batwin will deliver you a fine topaz. You will guess I am sure, what to do with it. One day we will meet again. Your loving friend, Pretzel."

There was plenty of Catoa and remaining birdseed, but the food smells continued to cause agonizing bellyaches as it took many days for Larrida to appear at the window. Little had Pretzel known that she had been sent to work in the communal kitchens for not smiling enough. As soon as Larrida was allowed to return home, Tarod showed her the note and they rushed to the window. They kept this a secret from the boys, not wanting to raise their hopes, and spent the night awake until they heard a small ping. Larrida tiptoed out to the balcony, wrapping the topaz in her scarf and barely able their excitement, waited till morning to wave to the little group huddled below.

After Batwin returned from his mission, Pretzel watched until Larrida, Tarod and their three boys left the balcony.

"We cannot wait for them. It could be many moons before it is safe for them to find a secret purchaser, a guard they can trust."

"A long wait," added Freya.

How could she ever forget the long incarceration in that tiny lice infested cage.

The wingflits all knew there were plenty of nuts as soon as they reached the forest. It was damper than last year, and Pretzel slipped and slid much of the way. The canoe became of use as shelter from the evening dew, while the wingflits perched on top. She enjoyed waking to the pattering of their feet above her.

As the shrubs thinned and the trees became taller, Pretzel knew it would be only a few days until they reached the River

Banzoor. She picked out a good wide branch to take with her, as Batwin queried its use.

"You will see before long."

When they arrived at the river, it was flowing faster than last year, and no sign of Harragar much to Pretzel's disappointment, but she chided herself. It was too much of a coincidence to expect her to be on the other side waiting with her mattress and broomstick.

"Roland, you could fly on and find Harragar, while I put my canoe together."

He flew off as the rest of the wingflits watched her fumbling with the struts.

"You must be so sorry for me having to risk my life in this."

She placed her baggage in the center and pushed off with her branch. The current was strong. It had looked so easy when Harragar swirled the mattress over to the other side, but Pretzel kept being swept downstream. Not to be daunted, she pushed off again and again until she managed to cross to the middle of the river. From here, she was carried by an eddy that took her to a small promontory of rock. How she wished she had large splayed feet like Harragar, who had so easily climbed the bank. With a great deal of slipping and grabbing onto whatever grass she could find, Pretzel dragged the canoe up to the same landing place where she had arrived with Harragar almost a year ago.

Roland flew down to her.

"There is no smoke."

Pretzel now felt sick with anxiety. Harragar always had the fire lit, winter or summer. She pulled out the pebbles of Vordak with trepidation. Surely they will show her to Harragar. She cracked open a pebble and stared into its depths. There was only blackness.

CHAPTER 27 THE SECRET OF HARRAGAR

Pretzel packed her stones away, feeling sick with anxiety.

"Fly back and search inside the house, Roland. She may have left the back door open; otherwise there will be a gap near the eaves where you can fly through."

Pretzel struggled to fold up her canoe, the wet canvas being more difficult to contend with, and kept dropping the bamboo struts as her hands were shaking.

It was not long before Roland returned and flew around her in frenzy. She had never seen him in such a state.

"Is she alive, Roland?"

"Follow me."

Pretzel ran despite her load as Roland led her past the house in the direction of the waterfall. His refusal to answer her question meant only one thing. The waterfall was flowing well. How she had longed to hear Harragar's cackle as she rode her mattress over that edge, but there was no sound bar the subdued twittering of the wingflits. Pretzel collapsed to the ground when she saw Harragar lying on her side at the bottom of the waterfall with one leg out at an awkward angle. She let out a scream and scrambled down the bank and as soon as she reached Harragar, tried to feel her pulse, but to her relief her chest was moving.

"Harragar! Can you hear me?"

"Water, girl! Just get me some water."

Pretzel broke down in tears and kissed the old lady's cheeks.

"Come on, girl. I am thirsty."

Pretzel laughed, despite the situation, for her Harragar was just the same old pragmatic self as always. She held her water bottle to Harragar's lips, who gulped the lot before ordering more.

"You can have the whole river if you want. What would have happened to you if I had not to come back today?"

"I wouldn't have lasted girl. The forest vultures would have had me for their supper!"

She tried to laugh but grabbed her chest.

"Oh, me gal!"

It was obvious now what had happened. Knowing Harragar, she would have wanted to make use of the waterfall after the heavy rains. She must have slipped when she climbed up back again with her mattress.

"I am weak now, Pretz. My ankle went snap and my old bones couldn't move me. What a ninny I am. But what a magniferous ride I had. The best!"

Pretzel laughed and cried for Harragar whose spirit that made her such a daredevil but now had let her down.

"How long have you been lying here?"

"Seems like weeks, girl, but must be a few days. Good thing it rained so I could stick my tongue out like a lizard and catch the drops. But the nights were cold as toads' backs."

She tried to sit up but fell back into a spasm of coughing.

"Time to get you up this hill."

Pretzel dragged the mattress from the river bank and shook off the caked mud before rolling Harragar on to it. She allowed frequent rests as each movement over the rocks caused Harragar to cry out. Freya remained by Harragar's side giving comforting twitters each time Harragar winced.

"What an amazing …little bird you are…Oh gollysnakes! My ankle!'

It was nightfall by the time they reached the top where Pretzel was able to drag her more easily into the house. Tachymus instructed the winglets to collect twigs for the fire, while Harragar leant back on her pillows to watch. Pretzel gave her what bread and butter she could find before straightening Harragar's ankle as much as she could then binding up it up with a strong scarf. She then found two branches that were sturdy enough to use as crutches. After putting some potatoes on the stove to heat, she sat beside Harragar.

"After our soup, girl, you must tell me all, and then there's to be no interruptions from you wingflits. Not even you, Freya."

However, as soon as Harragar had eaten, she fell into an exhausted sleep. There was nothing Pretzel could do but climb into her sac and try to sleep also, but she felt too excited hearing the old woman's breathing alongside her again. She lay there opening her pebbles and immediately saw the waterfall with Harragar dancing above it followed by her herd of goats and sobbed with relief at the fact her old friend was safe and her magic pebbles were working again. She couldn't wait now to show her old friend what she had brought back from Mt. Vordak.

At first light Harragar stirred. How could Pretzel forget? The old lady was always up at the crack of dawn and despite her ordeal nothing had changed.

"Hang on to my shoulder and put all your weight on your good leg."

Pretzel supported Harragar as they made their way outside to the wash basin, brought a seat out for her and helped her undress.

"I'm a funny looking old chook aren't I?"

Pretzel poured warm water over Harragar's mud caked hair, leaving it to hang down over her shoulders to dry, and kissed her.

"Harragar! You are the most beautiful woman in the entire world. You are like…a .how can I say it…a sculpture."

"I like that. Work of art in progress."

They both cackled. It was just like old times except that this time Harragar was thinner than before and her eyes looked as if they had a mist over them.

When they returned inside Pretzel helped Harragar back to her bed and waited as the old lady took her time munching bread spread thickly with butter and blackberry jam, savouring each morsel until she eventually patted the pillow beside her.

"Come and sit here, girl. Tell me all."

Harragar listened in silence, nodding her head at Pretzel's description of the mountain and chortled at her fear of falling into the abyss.

"What did I say? You just jump."

"I remembered what you said but I was too afraid, but I found that out in due course and when I leapt out the vines held me until I floated down. I landed in a basin with a cave and now see these. I have brought them to show you!"

Harragar took one of the pebbles to inspect, and then put it aside.

"Go on."

"Don't you want to open it?"

"Just go on, girl."

Pretzel felt surprised at what appeared disinterest in them, but continued on with her description of how the wingflits had brought a topaz to light up her way out.

"You see that, Pretzi? Do you see that you were not alone after all? No on really achieves anything alone. If they think they can take all the credit they can't."

"I know Harragar. I would not have managed without the wingflits… Batwin and…"

"So you climbed out and what then?"

"I left my flags behind."

"So how did you find your way home?"

"I looked into those."

"Oh, those!"\

Pretzel felt again perturbed by the strange look in Harragar's eyes, but enjoyed relating her adventures and her escape from the fisherman as she shook with delight. When Pretzel described her return to Grataco, Harragar pulled herself up and looked intently into her face and her voice became soft.

"And how was it then?"

"I don't belong there anymore."

"I thought as much. So be it."

Pretzel looked at her quizzically. "I had to come back to be with you. Grataco is no longer my home."

Harragar gave a sigh, "Girl, you have learnt much. But yet you have not begun yet to know anything."

Pretzel looked crestfallen.

"Come girl, I'll show you. Help me to the river, and bring your pebble things with you."

Pretzel decided it was best not to ask quiz her anymore as she could see the set in Harragar's jaw. It was time to be silent and wait. The wingflits followed respectfully behind them until Harragar turned around.

"Do something useful and collect us some berries. I can't climb that ladder like this!"

Pretzel felt cheered by the Harragar of old, bossing them round again.

"This is a good place as any."

Pretzel lowered her on to a flat rock. They sat in silence listening to the waterfall as Pretzel waited patiently, wondering what Harragar was going to say next. Eventually Harragar leaned across her to pick up one of her pebbles.

"What will you do with these now?"

"'You haven't asked me yet what they can do. Look! If I break one open you will be able to see things also. I know, for you have been to the Wattoo so you must have discovered them too."

"What will you do with them now," Harragar repeated.

"I will keep them with me forever and they will make me brave for I feel safe with them and what's more I can see things that no one else can so..."

"That makes you special?"

"I suppose so, Yes."

"So?"

"Well, it is important, is it not?"

Pretzel was beginning to feel more and more disheartened at Harragar's attitude. She had savoured this moment over and over in her head, relishing the thought of sharing her remarkable find and... it was like being teased. Harragar was behaving like Drako. She could not stand it any longer and stood up.

"Listen, Harragar! I found you, my flags led me to you and you showed me where to go next. I have returned with these wondrous pebbles that never let me down...well, only once and I thought you were dead, and now I have them and I am happy.

"But you were not happy. You left again."

"Because when I returned home, no one understood."

'What don't they understand, girl?"

"Me. My pebbles."

"So?"

"We both have found the secret. They do not know anything."

Tears rolled down her cheek as she sat down again and Harragar pulled her over to her and continued to stroke her hair but said nothing.

"I want to stay here for ever. Be like you."

"I am getting old. I will die here soon. No place for you here girl."

"Yes it is. I am happy here. I can grow vegetables and feed the goats and be just like you. I want my life to be the same as yours."

"Please yourself, girl."

Again Harragar became silent as the wingflits twittered in the background.

Suddenly she picked up all of Pretzel's pebbles.

"See these."

"Of course I see them! I have carried them all the way from Mt Vordak and home and now here for you to see them."

"Now, watch."

Before Pretzel could stop her, Harragar flung them down the riverbank as Pretzel screamed and scrambled down the slope in haste to retrieve them. To her horror there was a myriad of little stones smoothed by the stream and were a replica of her own. She picked up one after the other cracking them against each other in desperation.

"I can't tell them apart. Help me!"

Harragar shook her head and chuckled.

"Have you gone mad?"

"Come here, girl. Leave them be."

Pretzel was shaking with rage as she looked up at Harragar.

"Am I to climb Mt Vordak all over again to bring back more. Is that what your lesson is all about?"

"Sit here, girl."

Harragar patted the rock, as Pretzel slumped beside her.

"Listen, my girl."

"I am tired of listening."

"Just be quiet now."

There was just the rustling of leaves as Pretzel sat beside Harragar.

"It is all just the same as before."

"Listen to me, girl. These stones make you think you have special powers. Look at me. I am alone here. I thought I was above the world too. So while you were gone I threw mine away. And then, a funny thing happened."

The sun was sinking over the ridge and shone onto the waterfall making a rainbow, but Pretzel was too intent to notice.

"So what did happen, Harragar?"

"You will see."

Harragar continued to sit in silence. Pretzel could hear the old lady's short breaths in rhythm to her own. She began to see her village bathed in morning light. She saw Poppo following his goat herd up the hill. She saw Marthamum pouring milk into the skillet. She saw Drako coming up the hill from the village, followed by his possum dog. She saw the dark eyes of Buccasan.

Harragar sat, stroking Pretzel's hand." You know now, girl. You know."

The End.